FAIR WINDS
AND
FOLLOWING SEAS

FAIR WINDS
AND
FOLLOWING SEAS

by Riley Roberts

Writers Club Press
San Jose New York Lincoln Shanghai

Fair Winds
and
Following Seas

Writers Club Press
an imprint of iUniverse, Inc.

For information address:
iUniverse, Inc.
5220 S. 16th St., Suite 200
Lincoln, NE 68512
www.iuniverse.com

ISBN: 0-595-24783-0

Printed in the United States of America

For everyone who put up with me during the writing of this book;
(you know who you are),
and to my family, for continued encouragement.

Foreword

During the reading of a historical novel, many are inclined to wonder how much of it actually occurred, and how much was the product of the author's mind. In this book, all of the ships, political movements, and diplomatic events were real, and have been retold as accurately as possible through the eyes of my characters. The only liberties I have taken as far as the naval commands are concerned is to place my heroes aboard strategic ships at pivotal times. There is a real Ria de Arosa, precisely where I say it is, and the channel is, as far as I can tell, described accurately in terms of depths and dimensions, but the rest of the details regarding the little waterway have been invented. All of the historical figures mentioned in this work were actual people (including, of course, Lord Nelson).

The American Navy in 1801 proved to be quite difficult to research, as it comes across as rather obscure at times in some contemporary accounts. One of the most reliable sources I discovered in the gathering of information I undertook when composing this work was *The Navy: A History*, by Fletcher Pratt. Many details regarding Lord Nelson's life and personality were furnished by the British National Maritime Museum, and others were discovered in the pages of Robert Southey's book *Lord H. Nelson*.

To my friends and family go many thanks indeed, especially to those who sat still, nodded, and mumbled "mm-hmm" whilst I babbled incessant naval gibberish at them. To all my sailing friends, acquaintances, and fellow crew members I owe a debt of gratitude, including everyone I got wet while trying to capsize some small boat or other.

I realize that there is nothing duller than a long foreword to a short book, so I shall confine myself to what I have just said, and to this: many heartfelt thanks to all who made themselves a part of this book, whether named here or not. I could not have gotten this far without you.

Riley Roberts
August 25, 2002
Wheaton, IL

CHAPTER 1

✿

When northerly gales blow from the sea, the spray carries up over the stocky hills and long beaches to Boston, and the beech trees in the square heel and roll like masts, staring out upon the dockyards that line the fringe of the harbor. Fog rolls in early every morning, descending over the rigging of the grand, ponderous tall ships that ride to anchor in the bay, and settling over the waterfront piers. Water slaps and bubbles against the pilings, and seagoing vessels bounce, rock, and corkscrew at the uneven send of the sea under their keels.

I was walking down along the docks one such morning when I glimpsed a figure, standing alone on a pier, enshrouded in the early morning mist. I approached slowly. The man, his back to me, struck a match and laid it to his pipe, bringing it to his mouth as he did so.

"Sir?" I called gently. The head partially turned.

"Yes, it's me," came the reply. His voice was deep and rather raspy, due to long years of abuse in naval command. I approached still closer, and the stranger turned to face me.

He was old; not immensely so, but at least sixty or seventy. His white hair was neatly combed and swept back from his face, which was shaven clean. He had a respectable visage, that of a retired gentleman, and held himself with a sort of penetrating dignity, so that one could simply sense importance in his presence. He wore a navy-blue pea jacket and dark breeches with the accustomed stockings and black shoes. He was not in uniform, and I had never laid eyes on him before in my life, but I knew him instantly.

"The meeting, sir?" I said.

"Yes. Punctual, Mr. Roberts. I like that in a writer."

"Thank you, sir."

"Shall we begin the interview, then?"

"Certainly, if it pleases you, sir."

He smiled and removed the pipe from his mouth, extending a hand to be shaken. His grip was firm, his palm dry.

"I never used to enjoy the company of writers," said he with a little chuckle. "but now I seem to collect them. Your letter was among the first I received, so I decided simply to accept it. I hope you don't object to my odd choice of a meeting-place?"

"Not at all," said I, looking around idly. "It's almost worthy of the beginning of a book."

"That it is," he responded with a sigh. "Or the end. I've not been in Boston for so long. Not Marblehead in years. But at the promotion, I thought I'd return here for a time."

"Yes, sir. Congratulations, sir." The department of the navy had only recently instated the rank of Admiral, and this man was the first to be promoted to that rank. It was honorary, mostly; but I daresay he deserved it.

"Thank you. This bench, perhaps?" We had arrived at a little plank on stilts that looked out on the harbor. At my nod, he moved to sit down, and I did the same. He began the elaborately choreographed dance of refilling his pipe. I produced my little pad of paper.

"How shall I begin, Mr. Roberts?"

"Well, sir; I'm not sure. First off, I suppose: how did you get here?"

"I cannoned a lot of Spaniards, I sunk a large number of English ships. I captured forts, I won battles. Could you do me the honor of being more specific?"

I was silent for a time. Here was perhaps the greatest man I had ever met; a distinguished naval officer, as great as Nelson himself. I was privileged enough to interview him for a biography. What should I ask him?

I looked up. He was watching me keenly. The smoke curled up from his pipe and mingled with the fog. A ship's bell clanged out the watch nearby. At that sound, his eyes left me and drifted out to sea, and his thoughts went with them. In his pupils I could see a thousand sights associated with that bell. Suddenly he was in uniform again, at the height of all his blazing glory, and I could feel the thick, stinging smoke from the cannons burn my eyes, and I could hear the splintering crashes and screams as his broadsides mutilated the hull of his opponent's ship. He stood on the quarterdeck, proud, erect, and tall. The scene flashed once before me, and then he blinked, and the old man on the pier let his eyes drop. I knew precisely what to ask him.

"How did it start?"

"What?"

"That," I said, gesturing vaguely out to sea. "All of that. What was it that made you the man you are today?"

"I-I'm not sure I understand," he faltered.

"Why are you the first American admiral?" I whispered.

It suddenly made perfect sense.

"That was so long ago," he began, looking down at his feet. "Fighting sail was in its prime, then. No steamships as there are today."

"And yourself?"

"Me?" he looked up at me. "I was only twenty then, or perhaps a few years older. It was 1801, I suppose; the assignment that effectively began my career. I became a man and a sailor, a leader and a captain. Those were the best days of my life; the glory days." He paused.

"Start at the beginning," I said gently. "The very first."

"The beginning," he said thoughtfully, a pensive smile on his wizened face. "It starts so simply. It begins with a ship."

❦   ❦   ❦

"The glass, if you please, Mr. West."

"Aye aye, sir."

"Bearing three degrees abaft the starboard beam. I can just make out her colors; that's the ship."

"Yes, Captain."

"Trim sail and prepare to come to the wind. We'll let her catch us. Steady as she goes, Mr. West," Captain Wilson said, clapping his telescope shut and handing it to his first lieutenant. He studied the man. A good fellow, this Lowell West. Wilson had been watching him for some time now, and had taken a liking to him. A liking! Ridiculous. He loved the boy as a son. Showed real naval promise, too; a very capable young officer.

"Aye aye, sir," West said, then turned to face the maindeck from the taffrail, where he, his captain, and the other lieutenants now stood. "Ready about! Hands aloft to reef the sails!" he bellowed, and there was a flutter of excitement on deck as men leapt up the ratlines to the spars, like so many spiders on a web. "Helm's-a-lee! Quartermaster, catch her as she turns." The man at the helm nodded, spinning the wheel at the first lieutenant's command. West turned to Second Lieutenant Goldman. "Mr. Goldman, watch main and fore trim. Bo'sun, prepare to render passing honors to the incoming vessel."

"Yes, sir."

"Heave the ship to, if you please, Mr. West," the captain ordered.

"Aye aye, sir. Back main and stay! Get that sheet in!"

Already, the other vessel was gaining distance on them. She was only about a mile away now; soon, the stars and stripes, flying from her mizzen yard, would be visible to the naked eye. West glanced out at the ship. A merchant lugger. Positively tiny compared to the frigate upon which he was standing, U.S.S. *Nova*.

Nova was a three-masted, 36-gun American built and operated frigate, a gem in the sparse navy. She had been commissioned in 1797 and completed only last year; now it was early 1801. Recently, Tripoli had begun sinking American merchant ships en route to trading ports in England and the Mediterranean; the British and French were engaged in a life-and-death struggle, with the Spanish fighting alongside the "frogs". Apparently, the Tripolitans were concerned about preserving an alliance with one of England's adversaries, and were trying to prevent the Brits from acquiring goods that could be used to restock their extensive navy. Eventually, the American government had decided to act on these unwarranted attacks, and so *Nova* had been ordered to rendezvous with the *Maria*, a trading vessel, and to escort her to an English resupply port in south Britain. If the *Maria* was attacked and *Nova* had to step into the conflict, America would likely go to war with Tripoli.

"Sir, flag in greeting?" Goldman asked West suddenly, breaking his train of thought.

"Yes, Mr. Goldman."

"Aye, sir."

A moment later, the stars and stripes fell about three feet and then raised again, in salute to the *Maria*, which was now only a quarter mile away. The other craft echoed the gesture. As West watched, her topsail began to quiver, and was soon furled. The *Maria* spun on her beam and came to rest neatly alongside *Nova*, at a distance of about a cable's length.

A moment later, West saw the quarterboat lowered off the deck of the other ship, and her captain soon followed. As the boat began to pull through the choppy seas toward the *Nova*, Captain Wilson spoke an order.

"Bo'sun's mates, stand to attention. Render salute."

The quarterboat was now alongside; West could hear the unsteady footfalls of the merchant ship's captain as he struggled to mount the boarding rigging, and then the boatswain's whistles began to trill as his head reached deck level. West touched his hat in salute, and stepped forward. The navy demanded rapidity in all its many facets.

"Captain Hamilton, welcome aboard U.S.S. *Nova*. I am First Lieutenant Lowell West, sir; please allow me to present our own Captain James Wilson."

"My dear sir, welcome aboard," said Wilson, without missing a beat.

"Ah! Wonderful to meet you, Captain Wilson," the other man proclaimed. "I trust your voyage has been satisfactory thus far?"

"Admirable, Captain Hamilton. Now, if you will join me in my cabin…"

Both men, after a few more words of formal greeting, retreated to the comparative solitude of the aft cabin. West breathed a sigh of relief, and dismissed the hands to duty.

Walking briskly to the poop, he enjoyed the first moment of down time that he'd had for the voyage. He breathed the cool sea air and felt the breezes, surveying first the ship—with its spindly-armed capstan, weathered canvas sails, and pristine wooden decks—and then himself.

Lowell J. West was of about average height, with a slight build and a drawn, boyish face. He was just twenty-six, after all, and had seen action only twice before, combating privateers as a midshipman in a smaller vessel. Upon his promotion to the rank of lieutenant, he had been reassigned to *Nova*, and was glad of it. He loved the sea. He'd dreamed about it as a boy, and sailed it for most of his life. His father, whom he'd never known, had moved his family to the fledgling United States in the midst of the great revolution. Finding there the freedom and political independence that was not present under the monarchy of England, he'd joined the makeshift American navy; he had been a fisherman all his life. Unfortunately, his father had been killed by a stray musketball, leaving only Lowell and his mother to fend for themselves at home.

He wished he could remember the war; all he had was a vision of the redcoats marching into Boston and his mother taking him and fleeing. Better still, he wished he could remember his father, and his first home, in London. There he had been born, in mid 1775, and his father had gone to the colonies to find work. He quickly grew to like it there, and, after the revolution was underway, returned home for his family, having chosen to move them all to the new and promising nation that he felt was rising from obscurity. Ah, his father. Mother always talked of him now; she had never remarried, and still lived in the same little house in Massachusetts. After Boston had been retaken by the rebels, the Wests had returned home, where Lowell had eventually taken up his father's old fishing business. It was a living, but he dreamed of sailing the ocean as a naval man, with a real quarterdeck to pace, enforcing his orders with the cat 'o nine tails. So he had gone to school, enlisting as a midshipman at the earliest possible age. Someday, he hoped to be a fleet Commodore; unlike the English, the American navy had no rank of Admiral as yet. It was unlikely he would be promoted beyond lieutenant, though; he had no friends in higher positions, and possessed no influence at the War Department.

Lost in thoughts of his past and the dreams he held for his future, West did not hear the shouting until a moment after it had begun. When he did, he sprang to the mizzenmast on the fore part of the quarterdeck. Apparently, the foremast watch had started the commotion. All remembrances of his boyhood disappeared as he raised his voice anxiously over the din of yelling.

"Mr. Baddlestone! What do you see?" He cried, straining to see the man's figure at the crosstrees of the foremast.

"Sail on the horizon four points off the port quarter!" came the earnest reply.

A thrill of excitement rushed through West's body. A Tripolitan ship of war? It was a definite possibility. He snatched up a telescope and ran to the taffrail, raising it to his eye as he did so.

Yes, there she was, just over the horizon and closing fast. By the spread of her sails, she looked British—no, she'd been re-rigged. She was almost definitely a Tripolitan vessel, recently captured from the English, probably something around forty guns. West lowered the glass and spun on his heel.

"Mr. Goldman!"

"Sir?"

"Present my regards to Captain Wilson, inform him that sail has been sighted, and request his immediate presence on deck."

"Aye aye, sir." Goldman saluted and disappeared below.

West raised the glass again. There she was, and an eighth-mile closer than she'd been a moment ago. Must be making a good eight or nine knots. West's heart was pounding now; they would have no choice but to fight her. If they got the wind behind them, then they could probably outmaneuver her, pumping grape shot into her sides and masts. If the wind didn't back at least two points, though, the situation would be reversed, and *Nova* would be on her way to the bottom within an hour.

Goldman, Wilson, and the merchant captain suddenly emerged from the map-room door, each of them cursing under their breaths. Wilson approached his first lieutenant on the quarterdeck.

"Mr. West, clear the deck for action and prepare to engage the enemy."

"Aye aye, sir," West turned to face the maindeck. "Clear for action! Hands to the braces! Gun captains, prepare to load!"

"Set full sail," ordered Wilson, looking surprisingly calm.

"Lay aloft! Hands loose all sails!" West relayed. Somewhere to his right, there was a protest from *Maria*'s captain.

"My ship! I must return aboard. Call away my quarterboat!"

"Belay!" Wilson interrupted. "No time. She'll be upon us in a moment. The glass, Mr. West!" the captain extended his hand. West placed a telescoped in his palm, and Wilson brought it to his eye. "She's closing. I can see her gunports along her starboard side; nothing run out, though. Twenty-two a side, I'd imagine." Forty-four guns!

The unfortunate Captain Hamilton was currently shouting orders to his crew to remain hove-to, but ready to flee at a signal from *Nova*.

"Mr. West, prepare to come about," Wilson put in. Now the ship was ready. With her deck cleared, her gun crews set, and her officers alert, she was fully prepared to engage a stronger enemy.

"Come to the wind! Hands aloft to reef the sails! Quartermaster, keep your eye on her bows!"

"Aye aye,sir"

Nova's topsails fluttered momentarily as they were taken in for the turn and then released. Slowly at first, the bows inched round, finally steadying when the enemy was coming from head-on. Smartly done, thought West

"She's bearing sou', sou'west, sir," announced the quartermaster. "We're making eight or so knots, so we'll catch her soons' enough."

"Excellent," West said, raising his glass again. The Tripolitan colors assaulted his eye. The two ships were much nearer one another. He set the glass aside and glanced up at *Nova's* own flag, the stars and stripes, flying twenty feet above her taffrail. Good. Let the other ship's survivors tell their superiors that they were sunk by an American.

"Mr. West!" Wilson was issuing another order.

"Yes, sir?"

"I'll have the guns loaded and run out along the starboard side."

"Aye aye, sir." West repeated the command, and the air was filled with a loud scraping as the gun carriages were extended out of their gunports. The carronades had been loaded in an instant, the powder boys standing ready from the instant the deck was cleared. "Stand by to open fire!"

"Gun crew number one, put a shot across her bow!" the captain barked. Seconds later, there was a flash and an angry report as the cannon went off. Still both vessels advanced. Wilson waited, gauging his distance and timing carefully, and then—

"Mr. West! Come hard-a-port!" The tension was mounting.

"Aye, sir! Helm-a-larboard seven points! Present starboard side! Gun captains, wait for the order. I'll have any man flogged who fires before his gun bears!" *Nova*'s broadside would be to the enemy ship for only a moment, but it was a moment during which both craft could receive damage. Fortunately, though, it seemed that the Tripolitans had not anticipated such a maneuver.

As soon as *Nova*'s starboard and the enemy's were square, West raised his voice again.

"Fire!" he shouted, and instantly there was the ear-shattering crash of all of *Nova*'s starboard-side carronades going off together. The ship reeled slightly from the recoil of the first organized broadside. Over the next thirty seconds, the air was peppered with the noise of gunfire from West's ship. By the time the other ship had her starboard guns run out, *Nova* had passed her by half a cable's length.

"Come about, Mr. West!" said Wilson, pleased with the momentary success of the assault.

"Aye, sir." He gave the appropriate orders, so that *Nova* spun on her heel, and was now approaching the enemy from far astern. Beneath her aft windows, West was able to read: "H.M.S. *Holmes*, Spithead, England." It was as West had earlier suspected; she was obviously a recently-captured prize.

Meanwhile, Captain Wilson had a glass to his eye.

"We've scored several critical hits in her side and torn up her sails pretty well. Mr. West!"

"Sir!"

"Order the port-side guns loaded and run out. We'll try to dis-mast her."

"Aye aye, sir." West did as he was told. With the *Nova* approaching *Holmes* from astern, the port guns would bear on the second pass.

They began to glide by again, port-carronades blazing faithfully away. As West watched, the other ship's fore topsail was ripped in two, and her mizzen yard was shattered. One shot hit her critically just above waterline, where the sea would come gushing in with every plunge and lift the ship took.

As the smoke cleared from the quarterdeck and West was allowed to view the entire port side once more, he was shocked to find that *Holmes's* guns weren't even run out. There was no return fire. Surely they must have expected the Americans to come round again! Something had gone terribly amiss.

"Sir!" cried the watch on *Nova's* forecastle. "Look there, sir!" He pointed to the sky above.

West looked, and was momentarily puzzled. Their, soaring through the air towards the maindeck, was a large, ceramic ball, apparently catapulted by the other ship. This was preposterous! Ceramics used in place of grape shot?

Another ball caught West's eye as it was hurled from *Holmes*, preceded by an odd "pop". This was followed by another and another. West returned his eyes to the first cask, now nearly overhead. All of the officers and crew of the *Nova* watched it, dumbfounded. It was in the rigging now—

There was a deafening crash as the cylinder exploded, raining tiny fragments of lead down on the ship's deck. Several of the larger pieces were actually on fire, and one collided with *Nova's* fore stay-sail, setting it immediately aflame. Fragments of the projectile descended upon the deck now, forcing all the hands to duck.

My God, thought West! That was a mortar! He'd heard briefly before that the Spaniards had developed shipboard mortars to fire on other vessels, but he'd never seen them in action. This would not end well, he thought.

"Mr. West, get some men up there to extinguish our sails!" Wilson ordered, his eyes burning as furiously as the canvas. "I want every idle man at the guns! Keep those blasted twelve-pounders firing!"

Already, a string of men had climbed the rigging, and were currently throwing buckets of seawater over the flaming sail.

Then the second shell exploded, setting another sail afire and igniting the only unburned portion of the staysail. On *Nova's* quarterdeck, all was chaos as her officers ran to and fro, issuing orders and trying to get the bilge pumps on deck to help with the flames.

God! West thought again. This was absolute hell! Many things could go terribly wrong aboard a ship at sea, but fire had to be the worst. Any wooden vessel was the perfect target for flame, her decks and masts large, old and dry, and her sails and rigging waterproofed with whale oil. She would burn for hours if something wasn't done.

The next thought that shot through West's mind nearly sent him into a panic. The powder magazine! Six and a half tons of volatile gunpowder sitting just under deck level. When that caught, there would be an explosion strong enough to tear *Nova* apart beneath his feet. And there was nothing that could be done…

Or was there. West raced up to his captain and reminded him of the problem.

"God!" Wilson was positively pale. "West, I want you to do all you can about that powder. Get it over the side. It's a long shot, but it just might pull us through. Step to it, sir!"

"Aye aye, sir!" That was it. He had to do it fast. Incredible that he'd only been assigned to this ship a year before, and already she was in grave danger of sinking.

Now to business. Where would he find men to help him clear the magazine? Everyone was either transporting water to the steadily burning sails or manning the guns…

Guns. That was it! *Nova* had almost passed the enemy ship by a full cable's length, and the guns would soon be out of necessity until she could come about and continue firing. The gun crews were where he would find his men.

Fiery destruction rained down upon the deck all around West, as more and more shells exploded and he fought his way to the carronades. As he passed the helm, he heard another explosion and a loud curse from behind him. He spun on his heel.

The quartermaster had been caught in the forehead by a flaming piece of lead, and had fallen behind the wheel, leaving it unmanned. No matter. Shrapnel had set the helm afire as well, burning through the towlines to the rudder, rendering *Nova* un-navigable except by sail. He turned and continued in his previous direction, emboldened with a new sense of urgency as the ship listed heavily to port, groaning loudly as she took on water.

Projectiles exploded overhead by the half-dozen. More sails were on fire, and burning fast. It seemed that the mainmast itself was now aflame. Even if West succeeded in emptying the magazine in time, it was doubtful that this raging inferno could be salvaged. He was at the port-side carronades now, the squeal and rumble of the gun carriages outscreaming the rhythmic explosions overhead.

"Avast firing, there! All of you men, come with me!" West shouted, straining his hollow voice to be heard over the noisy din of battle. The guns crews abandoned their weapons and accompanied him to the open hatchway that led to the ship's powder stores. "We've got to get every grain of powder up from there before the deck catches fire! Two men to a barrel, now! Show a leg!"

The hands, grumbling audibly at this new task but sensing the urgency that necessitated its execution, descended to the magazine in pairs, emerging slowly with casks of powder. West ordered all of it dumped over the side. True, gunpowder was a precious commodity in the American navy, but ships themselves were in far greater demand, and existed more scarcely. It was worth the loss in order to save the *Nova*.

Five, six, seven barrels. Eight still to go. Slowly, the ship would be rid of this grave threat to her very existence. Suddenly, West heard a shout of alarm from behind him, and, turning, saw that a man had slipped while ascending the stairs with a cask of powder. Now half of its contents were spilled down the ladder. If that caught fire…

"Stop! All of you!" he hollered, then turned to face the quarter-deck. "Captain Wilson, sir!"

"What the devil is it, Mr. West?"

"Powder spilled all down the ladder, sir, at the forward magazine!"

"Damn!" Wilson cursed himself for the clumsiness of his men. The situation was grave, and now he would probably have to abandon ship. He should've given the order far sooner.

On the other hand, if they could escape *Holmes*' assault in time, they might be able to limp back to port to avoid sinking. If he abandoned the ship now, he knew, he would face court-martial for a charge of neglect in doing a maximum amount of damage to the enemy.

He surveyed his sorry deck. Long tongues of black smoke curled up from the wooden planking wherever shards of ceramic had started fires. It seemed that the entire compliment of sails was afire when he glanced aloft. He had to decide on a course of action.

He was never allowed the chance. As the hands rushed forward and aft with water and the officers shouted commands, one of the Tripolitan projectiles hit the deck and shattered without exploding, leaving a pile of smoldering powder very near to the magazine hatchway. Its fuse burned down to the explosive, and there was a sudden, violent flash of angry orange light and a loud report. Flame leapt in every direction, igniting the spilled powder from the magazine.

West saw all of this happen as he stood at the base of the mainmast, facing forward at her bows. As the fire flared up and roared down to the powder stores, he started to turn and run, but it was too late. Within seconds, the three and a half tons of gunpowder that had not been poured overside caught fire and exploded.

The sound was deafening as deck planks were ripped from their fittings and the foremast was blown clear out of its place. Beneath the waterline, *Nova*'s hull was ripped into two large sections, and her bows were lifted into the air.

The impact threw everyone on the forecastle over the side, including West, who was hurled over the rail just ahead of the blast. He was lucky. One of the midshipmen who had been standing nearby when the explosion occurred was impaled through the throat by a flaming splinter. Another lost his legs. Men were flung off of the ratlines as they combated the burning sails, and they fell to the flaming deck, where, after a sickening *crunch* and a splatter of blood, they were no more.

Nova was sinking fast now. Her bows had almost completely parted, and her maindeck was past the capstan in seawater. On the quarterdeck, Captain Wilson had regained his feet, and was now ordering remaining officers and hands to call away the jolly boat, quarterboat, and gig. Poor Captain Hamilton of the *Maria*, who had been forgotten as yet, was now seen to be floating, face down, in the heaving ocean, about half a cable's length away, surrounded by splintering debris.

Now the boats had been manned and lowered, and were paddling steadily away from the flaming wreck, plucking survivors out of the water as they did so.

When West had hit the water, he had immediately kicked as far away from the ship as he could, clinging to a piece of charred deck planking, as he was not a good swimmer. Within minutes, he was picked up by the quarterboat, and sat, shivering, next to the captain in the sternsheets of the little craft. Wilson had a wistful look in his eyes as he watched his ship go down; it was unlikely that he would ever be entrusted with such an important command again. The sea was creeping over *Nova*'s quarterdeck now, rising over the vacant helm. He stiffened slightly as the poop went under, and went entirely limp as the proud American colors disappeared beneath the waves.

Wilson turned and looked at his first lieutenant, who had done all he could to save the ship. It was possible that he would face a court-martial as well; if so, his career would be ruined. Wilson wouldn't stand for it, though. Even if *he* was left to wallow on half-pay, he would do everything possible to save West from that disgrace. Why, Wilson had friends in high places! Why not speak to one of them, ask them to exert their influence over the War Department in securing for West a respectable post? A chance to distinguish himself, so that *Nova* would be forgotten? Yes, yes, he would do that. West didn't deserve a court-martial; if anything, a promotion for his valiant effort to save the ship. There was Estleman. Wilson could make a recommendation to Estleman for a promotion to commander for West. That would work. It had to…and if not, the boy's future was ruined.

Behind the retreating boats, *Holmes* had gone about, and was now sailing in the opposite direction. She was listing heavily, and riding very low in the water. Apparently, *Nova* had affected just enough damage to make it inadvisable for the other ship to continue pursuit of the merchant craft or the other survivors. Good; she would be that much the worse for wear against the next American she ran across. Ahead, the *Maria* rode to her anchor about a cable's length away. The little boats would be hauled aboard, and then the long return voyage to Boston could begin. It would be ludicrous for the ship to undertake the remainder of her voyage without a substantial escort.

Wilson looked again at his senior lieutenant. Apparently, West knew what awaited him in port as well as his captain did, for the expression on his face was bleak. Ah, well. He would do all he could.

Silence prevailed, hanging thick in the air as each man reflected, waited, wondered, slept, and prayed.

CHAPTER 2

The months passed, and summer came and went. In August of that year, 1801, war was declared on Tripoli and the Barbary States, due to attacks on trade ships, and a tribute demanded by the Tripolitan pasha but unpaid by the United States. Now, ships clashed at every juncture in the Mediterranean, the British, French and Spanish, and now the Americans and the Tripolitans. Each day, exciting news of battles and captures arrived in the ports of Boston, where the great ships of the steadily growing navy returned for supplies and repairs. And West could see it all through his window, and it maddened him to be away from it.

He was staying at the *Old Boston Inn*, a little place at Marblehead Harbor, built mainly to cater to the officers and sailors of the navy that were constantly in need of temporary quarters on shore leave. West was well known there now, for there he had stayed for nearly six months, ever since the *Maria* had sailed disdainfully into port with news of *Nova*'s demise. There had been a prompt inquiry, which, to his great relief, had ended without court-martial. But that had done little to improve his situation. For six months now, he had been ashore on half-pay without commission, and for six months he had watched the increased ship activity in the bay through his little window. It was beginning to wear on his nerves. He waited, hopelessly, for new orders, but they never came. His uniform hung, neglected and gathering dust, in the bare closet.

A knock on the door roused the lieutenant from his pensive silence. That would be the landlady, old Mrs. Michaels, with breakfast.

"Come in, Mrs. Michaels," he said, greeting her as he did every morning. A little bonneted figure pushed the door open.

"Steak an' eggs, sir, like always," she said, thrusting a tarnished silver tray at him. She was a dumpy little person of his mother's generation, with a rather deep voice (for a woman), a chubby little face, and very yellow teeth, several of them missing entirely. West was neither endeared to nor distrustful of her; he felt nothing but vague indifference.

"Thank you, ma'am. I am hungry today," he lied. In truth, he was beginning to dislike steak and eggs, having eaten it every morning for nearly half a year. But he must humor her, or he could easily find himself out on the street with only his naval salary as a flimsy shelter for him.

Mrs. Michaels bowed clumsily out as he began to eat, an inexplicable queer little smile playing across her lips. West did not try to comprehend that smile, or the woman attached to it, for that matter. Once she had gone, he set the fork on the tray, and put it aside. Next would come his morning walk, and he would return to the room to find the day's mail on his little table, if there was any. There was usually a letter from his mother, asking him to come and stay with her, rather than pay rent "at a nasty little place like that one." West could not intrude upon her in that way; he knew how difficult it would be for her to have him about. As it was, he called on her at least twice a week, but she still thought him unhappy. He sighed, sitting back on the hard little bed that he'd grown so accustomed to. He *was* unhappy; frightfully so, and had been for so long. It seemed as though the navy would never call him into service again; the ships of war gliding gracefully past his window every day and the *Boston*

Naval Chronicle that he read every afternoon seemed placed there deliberately to taunt him, and to heighten his steadily growing sense of despair.

Perhaps he should tender his resignation, he thought. Perhaps another field would better suit him. If he could wait until enough money accumulated for him to buy a little dinghy, he could fish again, like he had just after the war, and his father before him.

Or perhaps England was his calling. He could say farewell to his mother and board a liner sailing for Spithead or Tor Bay. He was British by birth, and his accent, though slight, was still of the London area, and the Royal Navy would certainly welcome his service as a midshipman—

And then he caught himself. All of these useless thoughts of abandonment. America was his home, where he belonged. He could never serve a King, an ignorant fool born into a position of inalienable power without any useful knowledge in the world, so far removed from the people as to appear superior. He felt a certain pride in his British heritage, naturally, and wished he could do something to serve both nations. He could not. No; he belonged in the American Navy, however long it took them to notice him again. He would stay there, biding his time, until he could finally set sail once again for the country he loved on the ocean he loved.

He smiled to himself. There was his old resolve again, calling the reckless mind back to the present circumstances and planting it firmly there, causing him to think of his true cares and obligations, to himself, his nation, and his mother.

The days blended together to form one large, indistinct period of time. West slept later and later, sinking once again into a black mood of despair, and slowly losing track of the days—or possibly months—since his last hope of salvation had left him. He longed for the ocean, for the gentle Atlantic swell, and for the rise and fall of a naval vessel. He missed, too, the continuous groaning and creaking of a wooden ship at sea, the smell of the salt breeze, and, strangely enough, the bitter ship's rations of which he had become enamored. These were terrible times for an old sailor.

And then, one morning, he awoke suddenly, much earlier than he usually did. Something had changed, or rather, something out of the ordinary had woken him up.

It came again; a knock on the door. That was odd; it was 7:30 by his watch, and much too early for Mrs. Michaels to be serving breakfast. She must be calling for another reason. He sighed. Another dreary day of nothingness.

The knock came again. He had better answer the old lady.

"Come in, Mrs. Michaels," he called through eyes half-closed.

"If you please, sir," came the muffled reply. "This is Midshipman Wickes, sir, of the War Department. I've a message to de…"

"I'll be right there," West called, instantly awake. A midshipman? From the War Department? For the first time in months, he was happy—giddy, he thought. He must be going to sea again! Unless—

His face fell. It was possible that they were discharging him. He pushed the possibility out of his mind, trying to appear perfectly normal as he finished tying his robe about his waist and opened the door.

The fellow was surprisingly short, even compared to West's average height. He wore the impeccable blue uniform of a naval midshipman, with the red sash that indicated shore duty.

"Lieutenant West, sir?" the boy asked, in a quavering, high voice.

"It is I," he replied, trying to mask the violent struggle that was taking place within him to appear calm and relaxed. Imperturbable; that was the word he would use, yes. Imperturbable.

"Orders, sir, from the War Department. No return service requested." He procured an envelope, the familiar wax seal of the United States War Department emblazoned on its parchment face.

"Thank you, my good lad. That will be all."

The boy snapped smartly to attention, saluted, spun on his heel, and trotted off, presumably to mount some horse that had been tied up elsewhere.

As soon as the young gentleman was safely out of sight, West slammed his door and set to work on the seal. It was broken easily enough; inside, there was one folded piece of heavy parchment, inscribed with his name and rank. He pulled it gently open. The flawless handwriting of a naval clerk met his eye. Somehow, it was a comforting sight. West read it over hurriedly.

Lnt. Lowell West
Old Boston Inn, Boston, Mass.
Previously Assigned <u>*Nova*</u>

Naval H.Q., Hartt Yards, Boston
War Department of the United States
October 7, 1801

Dear Sir,

Upon receipt of this notice, you are hereby requested and required to accept without protest a promotion to the Honorable Rank of Naval Master and Commander, effective as of this date. You are to report to Hartt Yards, at Marblehead Harbor to take command of the Sloop of War U.S.S. <u>Perseverance</u>, at eight of the clock on the morning of October 8, 1801. You will find further orders awaiting you aboardships. The Department of the Navy extends its sincere congratulations upon your advancement of rank, and trust that you will execute the duties of command to the full extent of your ability, so help you God, and that you shall engage the enemy relentlessly and at every opportunity provided to you, in the Defense of a Nation at War.

Your ob't servant,
Commodore Charles Reid

He wasn't being discharged, by God! He was going to sea again, as a Commander, captaining his own ship, no less!

Why, though? His last voyage had ended in total disaster! He had been on half-pay for nearly seven months now! Why, at this point, was he promoted to Commander, entrusted with a ship of his own, and reinstated on full salary?

And then he knew: Wilson. Old Captain Wilson had felt sorry for him, and, (though he was never to know to what extent), had put in a good word for him with some commodore or other, not necessarily the one from whom the letter arrived. He was going to sea again, he was going to sea again!

The excitement welled up within him, so that he wanted to dance around his little apartment. Ridiculous, ridiculous. Enough of that. It was time for business.

For the first time in what seemed like eons, West rose from his seated position on the bed with a purposeful stride, blowing the dust off of one of his sea-chests and opening it.

Ah, there it was, to be worn for the last time. He picked up his cutlass, and, old and tarnished as it was, he cradled it as though it were a child. He'd had it for more than a year now, and, with the presentation of a nicer sword at his promotion, he would have to sell it. If he did not, there would be no cabin stores for his own meals and his guests'. Digging out his cocked hat as well, he donned the uniform, and stood for a moment, admiring himself in the mirror. Finally, after so long, he felt wanted again; his life now had a purpose. It was back to the navy, and this time, he had a quarterdeck to pace.

The last thing he took as he left the room was his money; all of it in a little coin purse, and that he slid into his pocket. Since he'd thought that half-pay would be his usual salary for quite some time, he'd cut back on a lot of his spending during the previous weeks, and now had quite a considerable sum in store. He would use it to buy a new uniform; his present one had nearly worn through. And after the uniform, there was one other thing to purchase: a certain item that he'd lost when the *Nova* went down, his treasured violin. But that could be dealt with shortly

Hailing a hansom at the street corner outside the *Old Boston Inn*, he proceeded to the Naval Department, and from there to the uniform shop. In less than an hour, he'd been outfitted with a new jacket, pea coat, hat, pair of knickers and stockings, shoes, pinchbeck shoe-buckles (he couldn't afford the silver), shirts, scarves, gloves, and a cutlass. The blade was of the finest engraved steel, while the hilt glimmered with pearl-and-diamond-encrusted gold. A fine sword if ever there was one. He received twelve dollars for the old weapon, which was more than he expected, and then he was done, leaving the little place feeling very dignified indeed, his left hand resting on his cutlass, his hat under his right arm, and a single gilt epaulette glittering on his shoulder.

"Where to, sir?" the coachman asked, answering his hail and pulling the horses to a stop so that he could climb in. He mumbled a reply, and in a flash he was off again, nearly in a daze as the fast-paced world of the United States Navy, which he had nearly forgotten, descended upon him once more, in full force. He spent the rest of that afternoon running between stores, getting prepared to go to sea again after so long, and writing a letter to his mother, whom he, sadly, had no time to visit before setting sail. She lived on nearly the opposite side of the city; it would be impossible for him to call on her in addition to doing all else that had to be done. He finally returned to the inn late that night, exhausted from a full day, stripped off the uniform, crawled between his sheets, and fell into a deep, dreamless sleep

CHAPTER 3

"Pull away!" West ordered to the boatman, taking his place in the sternsheets of the little shore dinghy. He tried to look as imposing as he could as the little vessel gathered headway, lifting his small chin and thrusting the epauletted shoulder forward with stern determination. With his fore-and-aft hat cocked at a rakish angle, he was quite a sight to all who beheld him. With a tight-lipped smile, he tried to imagine what was going on aboard his ship at the moment.

From across the harbor, the fore watch would spot the gig on its way out to the larger vessel, and would hail deck. The first lieutenant would be found and informed of the new captain's approach (though he held the rank of Commander, the honorary title of Captain was his, due to the post command he had). A glass would be raised for confirmation, the epaulette sighted, and all hands would be called for his coming aboard.

From the gig, *Perseverance* appeared gigantic, though she was only a ship of medium size in the navy. Her pristine decks, furled sails, and proud bowsprit gave her a sort of majestic air as she rode to her anchor. She was very obviously of British construction; a captured prize during the Revolution, no doubt. Though she was relatively old, she appeared to be in perfect working order. Her boast of twenty-two guns posed a threat to any craft, and, when combined with her size, speed, and agility, could prove quite deadly when up against a more sluggish foe.

The gig was drawing alongside now, and a hail came from the towering quarterdeck.

"Return hail, sir?" asked the oarsman, requesting permission to acknowledge that the fearsome figure perched in the aft section of the little boat was, indeed the one and only Captain of the *Perseverance*.

"Acknowledge," West commanded, trying his best to appear calm, though the excitement and nervousness were welling up within him uncontrollably.

"Come aboard, sir!" came the reply, once the oarsman had hollered his affirmative.

He dropped a quarter into the fellow's outstretched and expectant hand, and then set himself to the difficult task of ascending the ship's side. It was something he felt (and looked, he was sure) very awkward at, with the unsteady heaving of the two craft in relation to one another. Above all, he must make a dignified first appearance on deck.

When it seemed as though the gig and the ship were both rising together in the swell, he took a deep breath, exhaled sharply, and flung himself at the boarding rigging that led up to the deck.

The boatswain's whistles trilled wildly as his head reached deck level, and ceased when he pulled himself up and steadied his uneasy legs. Before him stood the ship's company at perfect attention; lieutenants, midshipmen, and hands, all there awaiting him.

For a moment, he looked about the deck. There were the three towering masts, sprouting yards at right angles and displaying impeccably furled sails; the stars and stripes flying proudly from the mizzen yard; the spindly capstan; lofty poop; and sprawling maindeck. It was all there, it was all perfect, and it was all *his*.

One man, tall and gangling, with bright eyes and a clean-shaven chin, stepped forward with a touch of his hat. This would be the ship's first lieutenant, West thought.

"Welcome aboard U.S.S. *Perseverance*, sir," he said, in a voice that West found unusually mellifluous. "I am First Lieutenant James Tallis, this is Second Lieutenant William Caswell, and he is Junior Lieutenant Jacob Nettleton."

West touched his own hat in reply.

"Thank you, Mr. Tallis. I am Commander Lowell West, appointed master of the *Perseverance*, here under orders to assume full command of the ship," he said, holding himself high and speaking the words that had been rehearsed more than ten times that morning. Once that performance was ended, he removed his orders, and, as was customary, read them aloud to the entire crew. This made the formal ceremony complete; he now had absolute authority.

"Sir, your sea-chests have been delivered aboard, and I have taken the liberty of allowing them to be stowed in your cabin."

"Very good, Mr. Tallis. How complete are her stores?" West said, indicating the yawning hatchway to the ship's hold.

"Well, sir," he shifted a little. "We are still in need of one ton further of salted meat, seven tons of water, and a magazine's compliment of powder."

"The shot?"

"It resides belowdeck, stacked next to the magazine with the cartridges."

Good, West thought. Shot was a great trouble to get aboard; he was glad that he wouldn't bear the responsibility of supervision for at least that task. As for his first lieutenant, the man seemed competent enough. He turned to face him once again.

"I hold you personally responsible for contacting the Victualling Yard and informing them of our needs. I expect we shall put to sea in less than a week, though I would like to be perfectly ready in three days' time. As for now, dismiss the ship's company to their duties. I shall arrange myself in the aft cabin."

"Aye aye, sir." Another knuckling of the forehead as a gesture of salute, and West spun on his heel and retreated, his cloak billowing grandly after him, into the aftercastle behind him. There stood a sentry, evidently one of the ship's marine guard, at the entrance to his cabin. He brushed past the fellow and, hearing the noise of the hands returning to duty, breathed a sigh of relief.

With the door closed safely behind him, West took the time to survey his quarters. The aft cabin was not a large one; but most definitely more spatially adequate than *Nova*'s wardroom, to which he was accustomed. It was sparsely furnished with canvas curtains, a small cot, several shelves, and a tarnished mirror and washbasin. In the corner, his sea-chests were placed side-by-side; there he would leave them for now. There was one thing in the room that made him inhale sharply; sitting on his little cot in the center of the room was a package of sealed orders.

Sealed orders! He had heard about them from his former captains, but never actually received any himself. They not only indicated the possibility of action in the very near future, but also spoke of an immense trust of him by the War Department. It all added up now! *Perseverance* was a very large ship for a mere commander in the navy; obviously, then, there was reason to believe that he had something special, something that stood out. Why not assign another commander, or a captain? Someone had obviously intervened in his favor, and West had already surmised as to who.

It was probable that the War Department, or perhaps a specific commodore under their instruction, was in need of a good young officer to take charge of a specific ship for a specific duty. Wilson, whom, West knew, had excellent contacts in high places, must have put forth quite a recommendation. The commodore had accepted this, ordered West's promotion, and assigned him the *Perseverance*.

But why that ship? It could be that a ship was required that could handle well, and had a great amount of firepower for its length and beam. That would make perfect sense, if a certain mission had to be executed on a shallow waterway, or along a coastline somewhere. Yes, he could be headed for the shores of Tripoli, to shell the—no, all of this speculation was pointless. He would simply open his orders; they would lay out the full situation before him. He approached his little cot, and, with a shaky hand, picked up the package and broke the seal. Two smaller envelopes presented themselves, one marked with higher priority than the other. This he took and opened, leaning over into the light of the stern windows to read:

Cmdr. Lowell West
U.S.S. Perseverance
Marblehead Harbor, Boston, Mass.

Naval H.Q., Hartt Yards, Boston, Mass.
War Department of the United States
October 8, 1801

Dear Sir,

Immediately upon receipt of these orders, you are hereby requested and required to ready your ship for sea within two days' time, and to set sail from Marblehead Bay on the instant of October 10, 1801, on a course to weather the western coast of Spain, and to proceed directly to the Bay of Biscay. There you shall rendezvous with the specialized and secretive Privateer Squadron, and submit to the command of Vice Commodore James Estleman for detached service. The full details of your mission shall be related in the second package of orders you have received, and which you are not to disturb until you have put a days' sail between your craft and the point of origin. They are of the utmost secrecy, and must be weighted and cast overboard once read and understood. The best of luck in this present venture.

Your ob't servant,
Commodore Charles Reid

West sighed disdainfully. He had gotten his hopes up, only to have them dashed to pieces once more with his actual assignment. He wasn't given to special duty! He was to spend the next months combating Spanish pirates in the Bay of Biscay, who, evidently, were harassing American warships en route to Tripoli, where the real fighting was going on. Wilson had recommended him for duty, and they had given him a larger ship than he deserved, but an unworthy assignment. Ah, well. His day would come. As for the moment, he would do his duty without complaint and to the best of his ability. What had to be done now?

To begin with, his orders to Tallis would need to be altered. He had told the man to be ready for sea in three days' time to sail in about a week, and now he had to depart in forty-eight hours! To business, to business.

As he strode up onto the quarterdeck of his ship, he felt a surge of pride, despite his dull first assignment. After all, he was in total command. The wind was in his hair, the heaving deck beneath his feet. He had been granted the freedom of authority, one which not many others would ever feel. After all, his orders weren't that bad. Privateers could prove very tricky; he had fought them before off the coast of Panama, as a midshipman. It was because of that duty that he could speak mediocre Spanish to date. At the thought of leading his gallant vessel into action, he felt true happiness as he never had before.

He surveyed his ship proudly: her three square-rigged masts stood with a majesty unequalled in any vessel but another man-of-war. He gazed up at the main top, resting almost three-quarters of the way up the mainmast. There were the futtock plates to hold the dead-eyes, the shrouds, and the mainstay. The entire platform was a little over ten foot wide, broken starboard and port with lubber holes for ascension. There were the cross-trees, spreading the main topgallant shrouds. It was all so familiar from his days as a junior officer, but somehow it was incredibly satisfying to look on it all again.

He cast his eyes to her deck. A water-hoy was alongside now, he noticed, currently pumping water into *Perseverance*'s casks. Every drop would be needed in the months ahead. And there were the lieutenants, standing on the maindeck below, directing the transfer. Tallis, Caswell, and Nettleton. They seemed fine men, but he would have to drill them and the rest of his crew extensively in the coming days. It put him at a disadvantage to be unfamiliar with his men, but that would have to play out as it did. Only time would serve him there.

"Mr. Tallis!" West called, attempting to look stern and yet kindly. There was the constant need to appear always calm, imperturbable, and above human discomfort to his men. Respect and admiration could be powerful allies. "If I may see you in my cabin for a moment?"

"Aye, sir!" came the shouted reply. A moment later, they were sitting opposite one another, with West's little desk between them in the cabin.

"I wish to revise my orders to you, based upon the instructions I have received from the War Department." He said.

"Indeed, sir?" Tallis said, with interest.

"We sail from Marblehead on the tenth. I want our stores completed tomorrow evening, and no later. At present, I am under careful instruction to keep any further information to myself, so I do not want my orders questioned." Actually, he was bound by no such code, but he felt it unprofessional to breath an unnecessary word on the subject.

"I understand entirely, sir. The commodore of the Victualling Yard has expressed his willingness to cooperate, so it shan't be difficult to speed things up a trifle. I'll have it done, sir."

"Thank you, Mr. Tallis. That will be all."

"Very good, sir," he replied, getting up to leave.

When the first lieutenant was back on deck, West rose and began to pace the length of his cabin. It would be good to have the stores brought on sooner, he thought, but Tallis could only push the Yard so much. Once aboard, they would have to be balanced out and placed strategically throughout the ship so that she would ride well in the water. Nothing must shift, nothing must alter its position in the least, or *Perseverance* would be liable to unbalance and capsize.

At seven bells, grog and rum was served as supper for the hands, and the officers dined as well; but the crew got little chance to enjoy it due to the arrival of the food barge. West saw the biscuits, salted beef, pork, lamb, dried fruit, and a small shipment of eggs and vegetables stowed away, and then the powder hulk came alongside.

The greatest caution had to be used in transporting the huge gunpowder casks belowdeck to the magazine. Working barefoot to avoid any chance of a spark, the hands slowly carried the necessary six tons of powder from one vessel to the other; the process taking the better part of three hours.

Soon, night had fallen over Boston, and *Perseverance* found herself shrouded in an impenetrable cloak of darkness. Once the powder hulk had pulled away, the shipboard lanterns were lit, and the hands looked to their new captain for the next order. West, who now found himself to be thoroughly exhausted after the full day of work, turned to Tallis.

"Post the usual watches, Mr. Tallis, and then dismiss the men to the 'tween decks. I shall retire now; name an officer of the watch and you may do the same. See that I am woken not after dawn tomorrow morning." With a touch of his hat, he spun, wrapped his pea jacket around him, and disappeared into the aft cabin.

The sun no longer streamed in through the stern windows, so the shadows cast by the flickering candles against the cabin bulkheads suggested the bars of a cage. Each of the corners faded into shadows eerily; it was a feeling to which he would become accustomed with time, though.

He had been the captain of the U.S.S. *Perseverance* for only a day now, but a lot had been accomplished under his careful direction. The ship was now possessed of enough foodstuffs and drinking water to last 132 days at sea; far longer than was likely necessary. Her magazine was full, her shot stowed; now there were only spices, cabin stores, rum, and livestock to load. That could all be completed within a few good hours of daylight the next day, and then everything would have to be shifted around until the ship rode correctly in the water. It required a delicate touch; properly done, it could increase *Perseverance's* speed by several knots, but carelessly attempted, it would decrease it by as much.

All in good time, thought West, reverting to the clichés which were so useful at times such as these. The next day would dawn soon enough—too soon, it seemed—and the one following would see him at sea again, and his top-secret orders opened.

Odd, that simple information regarding the sinking of privateers off of Spain would be treated so loftily as that; but no matter. The government could do what it would; West surmised that the wonderful freedom felt when in total command of a ship compared to nothing else the world over. Still, very queer…

Slowly, Commander Lowell West drifted off to sleep after a long day, wondering…

CHAPTER 4

The constant braying of the bullocks annoyed West entirely as they were led on board, by threes, from the Victualling barge. One animal nearly went overboard as it was chased about the maindeck by several very confused topmen, having broken the rope that bound it to its comrades. The rampage ended only when the wretched creature caught sight of the heaving sea overside, turned, and, in its blind terror, ran into the waiting arms of a crewman, who wrestled it to the deck and got another rope round its haunches. West watched the affair with a distinct disgust, directed neither at the men nor the animals, but at the prospect of wasting perfectly good sea biscuits on fattening useless cattle. The men wanted their fresh meat, he knew, though he would survive well enough on salt pork, gruel, and biscuits. More trouble than they were worth, he thought to himself, and he wasn't sure if he meant the beasts or the men. He knew the need of a happy, well-trained crew, and did not think badly of the hands themselves, but at sea fresh meat was quite a lot to ask.

Already that morning, the rum, spices, and cabin stores had been taken aboard; when the cattle were quartered, *Perseverance* would be ready for sea. An inspection of the ship and the men would be executed, and sail would be set the next day. Yes, thought West, there was certainly something to be said for naval discipline and efficiency.

He was proud of his crew; only anxious now to observe their performance aloft and at battle.

Slowly, ever so slowly, the animals were taken below, and, under West's watchful eye and Tallis's experienced supervision, the stores were temporarily secured. Now it was time to see how she sat in the water.

When the gig had been lowered overside and manned, West descended to it very carefully, and arranged himself in the stern-sheets.

"Pull out to half a cable's length away." He ordered to his coxswain, who responded with the customary "Aye aye, sir." This distance would allow him an adequate view of his ship's waterline.

Though the coxswain and oarsman had a difficult time avoiding collision with other watercraft in busy Marblehead Harbor, the appropriate distance was eventually achieved.

West marveled at her. She appeared to him more magnificent now than she had been only a day before. Though she was a relatively small ship in the naval hierarchy, she commanded respect with her sleek shape, towering masts, and twelve-pounders. Her yards lay impeccably crossed, ready for sail to be set; and her eleven gunports a side gave the elegant form a menacing quality. On deck, the hands were dining in comparative silence, while the officers sat together on the poop and conversed.

Her waterline was roughly even from bow to stern; she also didn't lay over to one side or the other. Tallis had done an excellent job regarding the placement of the stores. There was no visible problem in weight distribution; her handling should be excellent.

"Cox'n, return to the ship," he rasped, satisfied that all was well with his ship. All that was left to do now was to wait out the rest of the day.

Even before the pipes died away as he came back aboard, he was voicing his approval for *Perseverance*'s weight distribution. An audible sigh of relief was detected from Tallis. The day had not reached its end, though.

For two hours that night, West held drills and races to set and furl sails, starboard watch versus port watch. Port won an overwhelming number of times; now starboard had to swab the maindeck alone the following morning. The whole of the ship's company enjoyed the matches, however, with men and officers cheering together while hands, and even a daring midshipman, raced up the ratlines to set, reef, or goose-wing sails. It also provided West with an excellent way of getting to know his crew before going to sea. The men were experienced, the officers efficient.

Perseverance was ready.

⚜   ⚜   ⚜

Six-thirty the next morning dawned cold and wet; a thick fog hung over all of Boston. The activity in Marblehead Harbor proceeded as usual, however, boats skimming the water in all directions, sheer hulks moving about to ships in need of stores. Aboard U.S.S. *Perseverance*, the ship's bell clanged twice, and it was echoed by the other ships in the busy port. The hourglasses on all of the vessels did not run at precisely the same speed.

Captain West was already pacing his lofty quarterdeck; he had been up at first light. On the maindeck, watch was being called, while a water-hoy crept slowly by overside. In less than an hour, he would be under weigh, sailing for the western coast of Spain. If this fog didn't get any worse, he thought to himself. It was already so thick that he had to strain his eyes to see the forecastle of his own ship; her bowsprit was entirely invisible to him. Though he could hear the quiet sloshing of the ocean overside, he could not see its surface for the mist. It was a very eerie feeling.

First Lieutenant Tallis loomed up out of the fog beside him.

"Reporting for duty, sir," he said. The faces of all the ship's officers were visible only as dim blurs under current conditions.

"Very good, Mr. Tallis," West replied, looking vainly about him. The weather was unlikely to abate, and might even worsen, within the next twelve hours; now was as good a time as any for setting sail. Delay, as implied in his orders, must be avoided at all costs. The captain pulled his pea jacket tighter around him, seeking refuge from the unwelcome mist. After a moment, he spoke again. "How is the wind today?"

"Sou', sou'east this morning, sir. Good for sailing, I'd wager."

"Excellent." He paused. "Pass the word for the quartermaster." Now the entire deck knew that they were to sail within the hour, as the cry was taken up through the ship. In a moment, a stocky little fellow by the name of Foster presented himself on the quarterdeck.

"Take the wheel, Mr. Foster," ordered West.

"Aye aye, sir," he replied, doing so with a crack of his knuckles. There were excited whispers among the men.

"Mr. Tallis!"

"Yes, sir?"

"Rouse the hands. Look sharp about it, there!" A moment's pause.

"Crew awaiting orders, sir."

"Thank you. Hands aloft to loose the sails!" he shouted. "I want two reefs in the mains'l and fors'l. Set flying jib and sprits'l at full heave. Mr. Caswell!" West now turned to the second lieutenant as Tallis echoed his orders to the men. "Get for'ard. I'd like you to watch our bow clearance of the other ships in the harbor."

"Aye aye, sir," he bustled off.

"Two reefs in the sails you ordered, sir," Tallis said, standing before his captain once again. "Main royal and fore stays'l goose-winged, sir."

"Thank you, Mr. Tallis. Up anchor!" he dismissed him back to duty, then addressed the helm. "Mr. Foster, three points a-starboard!"

"Aye aye, sir."

Slowly, the ship gathered headway. As soon as he felt the rudder bite, Foster spun the wheel, and, more slowly still, West felt *Perseverance* respond. She crawled sluggishly away from her old anchorage, gaining speed rapidly under sail. Caswell hailed from the bows.

"Half a cable's length from U.S.S. *Connecticut's* starboard side, sir!" he called.

"Thank you, Mr. Caswell. Two points further, Mr. Foster. Mr. Tallis!"

"Sir!"

"Prepare to come about!"

"Aye aye, sir."

Perseverance was now moving at a good clip; evidently, from her smooth handling, the stores were well distributed. He felt the leap and pull of his ship, the creaking of her deck, and the very fabric of the hull itself gliding gracefully through the water. A sudden intense pleasure filled him at the deck's heaving; it was good to be under weigh again.

"Bring the ship about, Mr. Tallis," he ordered.

"Aye, sir. Hands aloft to reef the sails! Helm-a-lee, Mr. Foster! Steady as she goes." West could see his first lieutenant's eye following the progress of the half-enshrouded bows across the horizon, gauging his timing. Since little could be seen of the harbor around them, Tallis had to rely on his compass and his gut to put the ship on a correct course. He began to issue orders once again. "Unfurl all sail with reefs! Port helm a little, Mr. Foster. Very nice." And then, to West, "We have come about, sir."

"Excellent." He smiled for the first time in the early morning light. His ship was cruising well now, and still gaining speed, with every possible inch of canvas brought to bear. "Mr. Nettleton!" he said, suddenly recalling the name of his junior lieutenant.

"Yes, sir?"

"Take down this message and signal it immediately: U.S.S. *Perseverance* to flagship; am setting sail to join indicated squadron as ordered."

"Aye aye, sir." There was a moment's pause, and then an odd combination of red and green lanterns were suddenly illuminated at the mizzen top; in this fog, night signals were necessary if any message was to be understood. Another moment, and an answering arrangement of similar lanterns were sighted, far on the starboard quarter. Nettleton instantly began to read the signal in reply.

"Flag acknowledges, sir, and wishes us the best of luck."

"Very good. Acknowledge that last remark."

"Aye, sir." The configuration of lanterns was momentarily changed, and then all were extinguished. Once this was done, West turned to the first lieutenant once more.

"Mr. Tallis!"

"Yes, sir?"

"Wear the ship. Lay in a course to weather the northwestern coast of Spain and the Bay of Biscay."

"Aye aye, sir," came the reply, and then Tallis disappeared under a veil of mist to plot the path that would be followed. The entire ship's company now knew of their destination, though most probably thought that it was to be a waypoint to Tripoli in the Mediterranean. West sighed. He wished it was; but his orders were to obey, not to question.

The sun was rising now, releasing fleeting rainbows of brilliant light as it pulled itself free of the distant horizon and began to melt away the fog. Soon it was a clear, beautiful day, of exactly the right temperature. Overside, the Atlantic seemed to glow blue; that color against the dazzling white of *Perseverance*'s seething wake was magnificent. As West stood on his quarterdeck and breathed deeply of the cool, salty air, and felt the warm sun on his cheek, he realized just how happy he was at sea. *Perseverance* plunged gently through the waves, the sails slackened and then surged ahead, and West felt it was good to be alive.

Tallis appeared at his elbow, and instantly the moment was lost.

"The wind's backing a point, sir," he said. "I recommend we trim sail."

"Yes, Mr. Tallis. You are quite right." He replied curtly, irritated at the sudden intrusion. It was a good point, though; the ship was making a steady thirteen knots through the water; a sail might be lost if the wind continued to strengthen. "Two reefs in her royals, if you please, and goose-wing the sprits'l."

"Aye aye, sir," he responded, giving the appropriate orders.

Overhead, the ship's bell sounded four strokes, compelling the captain to issue another order.

"The hands will breakfast now, Mr. Tallis, and I will dine in my own cabin."

"Very well, sir."

West's personal attendant, a man called Sway, was an excellent cook. Breakfast that morning consisted of beef, eggs, and morning coffee, prepared attractively and tasting just as well. West devoured it in an instant, and then leaned back and sipped a second cup of coffee at leisure. He was finished by five bells.

By high noon, West had conducted two sailing drills and a quarters exercise. The ship's company supped soon afterward; more drills followed. He was working the men hard; the tension of the last few days of preparation made him uneasy. Though the orders seemed benign enough, there was something that didn't quite fit, something eerie, almost foreboding. It was probably only his nerves, but he wanted to be ready for anything all the same.

By the beginning of the evening watch, night had cast its slowly thickening shadow over the little sloop. Captain and crew alike were exhausted; the hands were dismissed to the 'tween decks, the officers to the wardroom and mess.

Another long day concluded, West picked his way back to the aft cabin under cover of darkness. At sea once again. It was a good feeling to be in command, and he hoped all would go as well for the rest of his commission. And then he remembered: orders!

Leaping from his cot to his desk in a single stride, he snatched up the remaining envelope, sealed with the wax eagle of the War Department. Opening it hurriedly, he emptied its contents into his lap: two sheets of heavy parchment.

The first was simply a restatement of the orders he'd already had, and he read through it once more, to provide a backdrop for the information he was about to receive. The second sheet, he found, was carefully folded, and sealed just as the envelope was. He broke the seal. Despite his boredom with the assignment that he'd been given, his hands shook violently as he unfolded the notice.

Cmdr. Lowell West
Cptn., U.S.S. Perseverance, at sea

Naval H.Q., Hartt Yards, Boston, Mass.
War Department of the United States
October 10, 1801

Dear Sir,

You should now be precisely one day out from Marblehead at this point in your voyage, with no enemy vessels in sight. If present conditions differ, read no further, and replace these orders in their envelope and then into a locked cabinet until all above conditions are met.

In accordance with your last dispatches, you should have set a course to weather the northwestern coast of Spain and departed this 10 of October 1801. If this is not the case, do so now. When you reach the above destination, you shall be met there by Vice Commodore James Estleman, of the Privateer Squadron. You are to submit to his command and follow his orders exactly.

*__The following content is of the top secrecy, and not to be dis-
closed to any person, ally or enemy, aboard, ashore of, or met by,
your vessel. The penalty for violation of this creed is death, as
stated outright in the Articles of War.__*

*The so-named Privateer Squadron is meant to mislead any person
overhearing its call. It is not, in fact, a detachment of ships with the
purpose of combating privateers. Recently, however, Spanish ships
based in the destination bay have been attacking American warships without cause or declaration of war. This is strictly against the
Articles of War, and must be ended immediately. If the general public of either country is to hear of the said attacks, war will be
declared, a war in which we do not possess resources enough to pre-
vail. As it currently stands, the War Department seeks to forcibly
bring about the cessation of this harassment without attracting
undue attention. Thus, the duty of the Privateer Squadron is to
incapacitate the involved factions of the Spanish navy. We suspect
that an entire shipyards and headquarters somewhere in the general
region of Biscay is devoted to our harassment; this must be incapacitated. If the squadron is not entirely successful in its endeavor, this
country will likely declare a state of war with Spain, and thus with
France as well.*

The best of luck to you and your men, Commander West.

There followed a salutation and signature similar to those earlier
received. The only remaining page in the heavy parchment envelope
simply contained vague instructions to weight and sink the orders
once they were understood.

That was it! That was the thing that didn't seem right! God,
thought West. It was completely different from everything previously indicated, by note or word of mouth. Monotonous privateer
duty! Weeks of boredom! He was being entrusted with privileged
information and a commission of "the top secrecy". Excitement
welled up within him, finally overflowing as he rose to his feet and
began to pace rapidly back and forth in the small cabin, his heel

brushing the foot of the stern windows as he turned at the one end, his toe against the door as he came to face the other.

West's mind raced as his thoughts passed rapidly, one to the next. Half an hour was past in a moment. Every eventuality, each and every detail that came to mind, was thought out carefully, the finished solution mentally placed aside, for use when and if the time arose. There were the chases to manage. It was likely, pursuing warships, that his deck would be cleared for action for hours at a time prior to battle, if not for entire days. Since, during that time, the galley fires would be extinguished, no hot food could be served during that time. Spare iron bracings would have to be heated prior to action, then, to afford his men the luxury of hot food at sea. A well-fed crew was a happy crew, and an energetic one.

For more than an hour and a half, West paced to and fro, his brain picked entirely apart with plans and ideas for the coming weeks. When he finally checked his watch again, it was well after midnight. So thrilled was he with the abrupt change of plans that he desired to act immediately. He opened his cabin door and spoke to the sentry there located.

"Pass the word for Mr. Tallis," said he. The sentry, after recovering from his mild surprise at the captain's consciousness, took up the cry.

In ten minutes, a bleary-eyed first lieutenant appeared, obviously freshly woken.

"You wish to see me, sir?" he droned.

"Yes, Mr. Tallis," West spat, hardly able to contain his excitement. Evidently, Tallis caught the gleam in his captain's eye and the strain in his voice, for he brightened a little. West continued. "I have opened our sealed orders."

"Indeed, sir?" Tallis was now wide awake, and for it no better at mastering his excitement.

"Yes." West tried, probably in vain, to sound indifferent. "As to their precise content, I am not at liberty to speak. But there is some information to which you are entitled, and which is necessitated by your post." He filled the man in on the true purpose of their assignment, omitting the details of the mission on the Spanish side of things; tidbits such as the possible existence of a specially dedicated shipyards and the imminence of war. There was a dual purpose here satisfied; secrecy was maintained, and he remained aloof and all-knowing; a necessity in the modern navy to all captains. If the men, even the officers, were allowed the knowledge of precisely what the orders were, they would worry and fret about everything, and the anxiety would show in their actions. In extreme cases, if an officer should strongly disagree with a step taken by the captain because that officer was overinformed, mutiny would become a concern. Blind trust was also a side-effect of this "underinformation"; the men would grow to love a captain they must follow without full knowledge. When West had finished his explanations, Tallis remained silent in awe at the immensity of the task at hand, and the power of his captain; it must be a truly great man that is trusted to such a daunting task by the War Department.

As for West himself, he had no idea why he, of all the worthy souls on the captains' list, had been chosen for such an important duty. He was certainly not a "truly great man," but there must be some reason that the decision had been enacted in his favor. This he would puzzle over for many a night following.

"As for the present," West continued finally, after letting the silence wear on for a moment, "I want the watches doubled the moment Spain is in sight. Is that quite clear?"

"Of course, sir."

"Very good. You may retire—but, as you do, please send a hand back to me with a twelve-pound cannonball and a small canvas bag."

"Aye aye, sir."

"That will be all, Mr. Tallis."

"Thank you, sir." With a touch of his hat, a short bow, and the slam of a door, he was gone.

Again, West felt his heart leap at the new assaignment. Apparently, old Captain Wilson had thought very highly of him indeed. The prospect of adventure made him positively jump with excitement.

There was a sudden sharp tap at the door as his thoughts were interrupted by a crewman with the requested supplies. H delivered them to his captain and ducked out quickly.

West replaced the dispatches in their envelope and slid them into the canvas bag. After placing the cannonball in with it and tying the bag shut, he donned his cloak and hat and went on deck. Evidently, the second lieutenant was officer of the watch. West approached him, startling the young fellow as he loomed out of the darkness at his elbow.

"Mr. Caswell!"

"Sir?"

"Is the horizon clear?" A pause.

"I believe it is, sir."

"I do not care what you *believe*, lieutenant; is or is not the horizon clear?"

"It is, sir."

"Thank you, Mr. Caswell." West walked to *Perseverance*'s taffrail, slowly extended his arm, and unceremoniously dropped the parcel into the little ship's wake. For a moment he remained there, watching it, until the powerful Atlantic closed over it. That was that; the government's secrets would be kept.

"Mr. Caswell."

"Yes, sir?"

"What is the sailing time to the Bay of Biscay?"

"About three more days, sir."

"I see." He paused. "Inform your superior when he relieves you that I wish him to drill the men in close-quarters battle tactic. Tell him to inform me of the success rate."

"Aye aye, sir. I'll pass it on to Mr. Tallis."

"Carry on, Mr. Caswell."

"Yes, sir."

The masthead watch would have heard the entire conversation; that was good. When he gossiped it all to the rest of the crew, it would set the men on edge. Three days' time was not enough, West knew, to be fully comfortable with his men as yet, but it would do to be as ready as possible for action.

With a last look around the deck and a swish of his boat-cloak, West spun on his heel and disappeared down the companionway. He slept well; it was the last time he would for weeks.

That day and the next seemed to roll by very slowly; the usual shipboard activities were seldom enough to occupy the mind. Only the promise of excitement with the Privateer Squadron kept West functioning; otherwise, the boredom would've been immense. For the men it wasn't nearly as bad. Constant drills served to keep them on their toes; the frequent ragged crash of a hundred tons of metal being run outboard for firing assaulted the ear constantly. Navigation classes for the officers by Caswell while Tallis drilled the hands; lead castings and sail drills for the off-duty watch. Every soul aboard was occupied except for the captain; West spent his days pacing the quarterdeck, attempting not to appear anxious, and keeping a close eye on Tallis, trying to find some minor error to pounce upon. There were none, however, and, as West lay in bed both nights, he was ashamed of himself for attempting to take out his boredom on his worthy first lieutenant. He was a fully capable officer; West tried to imagine the hurt look he would receive if he were to pick the poor man apart before the entire ship's company. True, wars could not be won without someone's feelings hurt, but discipline and cause for mutiny could never be confused.

The third day dawned cold and clear; the very climate itself felt new and refreshed. West was glad of the change from the first minute he awoke.

The usual creaks and groans of a wooden ship at sea complimented the lazy sighing of the ocean as *Perseverance* rode the waves.

An ominous tension hung in the salty air, its breeze stirring the sails and returning life to the ship.

West was on deck with the sun, scanning the distant horizon for land or sail. Now it was clear; in only a few minutes the Privateer Squadron could be in sight.

As he paced the length of the quarterdeck (as he did nearly every morning), he thought of the battles that awaited him. In all the thought he'd given to the action he would soon see, the grisly details of war never came to mind. A few days might see him as a mutilated corpse lying on this very quarterdeck, his insides spilt all down the side of the ship. He could be injured or killed at any moment, and still he was recklessly excited at the prospect of battle looming in the near future. He had to be careful to slow his nervous strides to casual steps as he walked along.

"Deck there!" came a yell from the masthead. "Sail-ho! Two points off the port bow!"

West stepped forward calmly, trying hard to sound unemotional.

"Thank you," said he. "Mr. Caswell, ascend the ratlines if you please."

"Aye aye, sir."

The hourly casting of the log would have to be postponed to determine the nature of the oncoming ship. It could be friend or foe; Spanish or French ships would likely fire on him, Tripolitans certainly would. If she were British, though, he would have nothing to fear. The second lieutenant was now hailing from the mainmast.

"She's there, sir!"

"What do you make of her?"

"Not sure—she's a good three hours out, though. Courses and topgallants, close-reefed. I—I'm afraid I haven't made myself familiar with this type of craft." The boy sounded very apologetic; West was sure that if his face could be seen from deck, the cheeks would be slightly red with an ashamed blush.

West sighed with annoyance. The second lieutenant of a sloop of war should be well able to identify all possible types of enemy craft. Still, this fellow could not be expected to know all of that at a moment's notice, and, without practical experience in that area, could not be blamed for his incompetence. In order to save the man from further embarrassment (and, West realized, to satisfy his own curiosity), he made a decision to view the incoming vessel himself.

"I'll come," he called. "A glass, Mr. Tallis. You have charge of the deck." West began to stride to the main shrouds, telescope in hand. He pulled himself up onto the ratlines.

He ascended slowly and shakily, listening to the wind singing through the rigging and the timbers of the ship creaking with every swell far below him. He was not nearly as sure of himself aloft as some of the hands were; even as a midshipman, he had dreaded the thought of ascending more than a dozen feet, and always did so with a slow step. Finally, more than a hundred feet from his quarterdeck, he pulled himself up to the masthead and stood, clinging to the mast, as the rise and fall of the ship swung him in wild circles. The swell was actually relatively mild today; he could only imagine what it must be like for the hands in a gale. And yet still they flew upwards in the ropes, skipping across the yards as though performing a strange aeronautical dance. Around him now, the sails filled and slackened, slackened and filled as the wind fluctuated and the sun shone. He steadied himself and whipped the glass to his eye.

On the horizon, he could just see the cut of her reefed topgallants as she bore down on them; by their spread, she could well be Spanish. British was slightly less likely. Although the King's ships were innumerable, their activity was concentrated now at the blockade of Ushant and at Sicily, not south near Bilbao. Yes, she was almost certainly a Spaniard. That meant action.

Beside him, Caswell stood roughly at attention, waiting for dismissal. West only just remembered to give him permission to return to the deck before he began to descend himself.

At deck level a few moment's later, West replaced the glass on its peg and turned to Tallis.

"The hands may dine now, Mr. Tallis," was all he said. "We shall confront the enemy in three hours' time." He knew that all idle hands had heard this statement, and it would serve as an encouragement and a warning to them. Patriotism, patriotism.

West had a hard time eating his dinner at a reasonable pace, for want of rushing on deck to see the ship's progress across the distant horizon. That would be impossible; such a rushed manner would be a public admission that he was tired and anxious. Instead, he forced himself to consume food slowly, attempting to appear relaxed as Sway poured his wine. He took a last bite and rose, telling himself that he'd eaten well, and made for the door.

The hands and officers had finished their meal moments earlier, and were now awaiting their orders. West took his place on the quarterdeck, just aft of the helm.

"Mr. Tallis!"

"Aye, sir!" He was doing a poor job concealing his excitement.

"Beat to quarters, if you please, and clear the deck for action. Do not trim sail until I give the order."

"Aye aye, sir." He began to give the appropriate orders.

Soon, the bulkheads had been torn down, the galley fire extinguished, and the deck swabbed, as was routine with that order. As the snare drums rolled and the boatswain's whistles pealed, Tallis turned to his captain.

"Deck cleared for action, sir."

"Thank you, Mr. Tallis. I'll have her guns loaded and run out along the port side."

"Aye aye, sir."

It was probable that that was where the Spanish ship would be passing her, and where the first cannon broadside would be affected.

"Guns loaded and run out, captain."

"Very good, Mr. Tallis. Double the watches and have the gun crews remain at attention."

"Yes, sir."

The enemy was visible from deck now, and with a glass it was determined that she did, indeed, fly the Spanish colors from her mizzen yard. *Perseverance* lay over to the wind, close-hauled on the port tack, ready to meet her foe.

Slowly, the ships inched toward one another; it seemed the other was a rather sluggish frigate, probably something around forty guns. That put them at a slight advantage, though *Perseverance* was undoubtedly much faster and certainly more maneuverable. The wind increased, the vessels moved still closer.

"Trim to battle sail, if you please, Mr. Tallis." The tension hung thick in the warm, salty air. Waves broke lazily against the ship's side as she tore through the Atlantic.

"Aye aye, sir."

The ships move forward still. Adrenaline suddenly flooded West's system; shadowy suspicions sprouted to doubts in his confused mind. What if he were to die? Or, worse yet, to fail? What if his ship were sunk, but he managed escape? He would be a disgrace, a laughingstock. The navy would never post him as a captain, and his crew would all be ashamed. What if he were to be horribly mutilated? Crippled? The War Department could do well without crippled commanders as captains! If his vessel were lost, court marshal and official reprimand would ensue. He would never be able to bear any of it!

He fought down the panic that was rising inside him, and turned his face and his thoughts to happier subjects. On deck, anxiety was running just as high; the gun crews were chattering away loudly at their stations. Ah, now there was something to distract him. Such noise was unprofessional; it must be stopped. His tortured consciousness eased when presented with this fresh task.

"Silence!" he roared, trying to seem imposing. The talking died away. West took a deep breath of the ocean air, and instantly found himself calm and battle-ready.

"Helm-a-lee, Mr. Foster! Steady as she goes. Mr. Tallis!"

"Sir?"

"Take charge of the guns."

"Aye aye, sir." He strode to the maindeck. The Spaniard was well within a cable's length now. The moment that West had prepared for for days was upon him. He felt the necessity of making the first move. It was now or never.

"Hard-a-starboard! Mr. Tallis, the twelve-pounders!"

"Aye aye, sir!" he paused, gauging his timing. The huge Spanish ship was very near now, so that officers could be seen standing aboard her quarterdeck, and hands manning her huge twenty-four pound guns.

"Fire!" Tallis suddenly shouted, and *Perseverance*'s guns vomited smoke and flame in unison. Splinters flew on the Spanish ship as smoke billowed off of the attacker's gundeck, and her quarterdeck lurched suddenly beneath West at the huge recoil. From overside, the screams of the enemy's wounded could be heard.

Then the Spanish ship let loose her first broadside. An ear-rending crash of guns, and West was instantly blinded by the gunsmoke that had been blown across his ship from the other. When it cleared, *Perseverance* had been transformed.

Wounded men, and perhaps a few dead, lay near the base of the mainmast, where they were quickly dragged in an endeavor to keep the guns clear. Now the *Perseverance* was returning fire; some gun crews reloaded faster than others, so the shots seemed nearly constant. His ship's deck was peppered with grape shot, but so was the other's. As yet, neither seemed to have a great advantage—*Perseverance*, as he had earlier thought, was perhaps reacting more rapidly—but the outcome of the battle was not clear-cut. In the terrible din of battle, West struggled to keep his head and began barking orders.

"Mr. Tallis! Wear the ship!" he cried, in a vain attempt to be heard. Tallis must have understood, though, because West could see his smoke-streaked visage give a nod. Both ships were now blasting away relentlessly; a foot-long wooden splinter rocketed past his head as he continued. "Prepare to come about! All guns loaded and run out! See that the wounded are taken to the cockpit, and keep those blasted guns firing!"

"Aye aye, sir!"

"Mr. Caswell!" And so the orders continued. Soon, *Perseverance* was coming round to her enemy's stern for another volley. Eleven carronades on her port side pounded unremittingly at her adversary's mere two; the bulk of the Spaniard's firepower was on her sides, not her ends.

As West watched, a promising young midshipman dissolved into a horrible red mass as he was flung across the deck by a twenty-four pound ball. The guns' crews strained to no end at the tackles, whilst the heave of the ship against the recoil of the carronades threatened to throw each man from his feet. They sponged and rammed, sponged and rammed the barrels of the guns. The next organized broadside crashed out rather raggedly as smoke poured from the ship's sides, and as the ocean surge bade fair to send each man reeling. Still they battled, and still they rallied behind their captain.

For West, the screams of the wounded were drowned out by the constant roar of the starboard-side quarterdeck carronade. He saw the splintering wood and the blood, however; now the enemy's side was within firing range, and fire the Spanish did. The ships were exchanging broadsides evenly now, raining iron hail upon each other's decks as they circled round in the open sea. Aloft, holes were appearing in sails by the dozen. Lines were cut by whistling cannonballs, and the rigging soon hung in tatters. On deck, crashes of wood and crunches of bone were all that could be heard aside from the rhythmic drone of the guns.

"Get that wounded man out from under the gun!" West found himself hollering, noticing trouble at the nearest cannoning station when the constant cycle of *squeal, bang, squeal*, as the gun was run out, fired, loaded, and run out again, was interrupted quite suddenly. There was an agonized scream, and then the carronade resumed its normal operation. "Very good. Now keep that time! Hands to the braces on the starboard side, there. Mr. Caswell, the powder monkeys!" West realized with a start exactly how strained and anxious his voice was sounding. Indeed, his body was very tense. He rolled out his shoulder muscles in an attempt to relax and resumed issuing orders. Even in the constant hell of battle, he thought ridiculously, he must appear cool, clairvoyant, and largely unemotional before his men.

"Try to dismast her!" Tallis was yelling. "Aim for her sails, her sails!" The guns fired, fired again.

And then, as if by a miracle, West saw the Spaniard's mainmast dip, straighten, dip again—a twelve-pounder from the *Perseverance* had found its mark! He heard frantic screaming in Spanish, sounding very distant, and saw the ship's officers rushing forward, barking orders. Slowly, it seemed, and with the grace of a ballet dancer, the mast toppled and fell overside. If the wreckage could not be cut away soon, it would act as a vast sea-anchor, leaving the vessel helpless.

Around him, the crew began to cheer raucously. Elation consumed even his officers, who began to leap up and down on the quarterdeck. Without a mainmast, the other ship's speed under sail would be cut nearly in two, leaving her prey to further crippling broadsides from the *Perseverance*. Reluctantly, West allowed himself a smile. It was good to let the men know that their captain could be human in such situations.

A cannonball whistled by West's ear, abruptly calling him back to the reality of the situation. Now was the time to act; the battle wasn't won just yet. He knew that dozens of his brother captains would sink her immediately with continued broadsides; but that was what the Spanish would be expecting. A better option came to mind.

"Mr. Tallis! Prepare to come about. Keep her guns firing all the while." The Spanish guns had ceased their bombardment in order to concentrate on hauling the wreckage back aboard enough to cut it away.

"Aye aye, sir." Evidently, from the look on the first lieutenant's face, Tallis was expecting West to continue the cannon broadsiding as much as the Spaniards were. West smiled wryly. Now it was time to give the order that would reveal precisely what was to happen. The bows crept across the horizon until they once again faced the enemy ship.

"All hands! All hands!" West commanded, at the top of his lungs. "Pistols and cutlasses, men!"

A cheer rose from amidships as the entire crew clamored over the maindeck to the armaments locker to equip themselves.

"We have come about, sir." Tallis reported, his voice quavering at mere thought of the battling that was to ensue. He had finally put the pieces together: West was going to board the enemy vessel.

"Thank you, Mr. Tallis." Now they were coming hard down the Spaniard's starboard side, very close to her railing. *Perseverance*'s crew would have to make that little leap between ships with the guns still blazing away; if West allowed the firing to stop, his adversary would certainly guess what was to actually take place. The hands were now running up the main shrouds to take in the sails.

Slowly, West drew his own cutlass from its sheath on his belt. It was a beautiful weapon with a golden hilt, a blade as new as this, his first command. He steadied his hat on his head and watched the two ships draw closer together. Now the bows were almost colliding; now the forecastles passed side by side. Yard after yard of the enemy's deck slid by; finally the captain could take it no longer.

"Sails furled! Over the side, men!" West shouted, letting out a savage yell that was taken up enthusiastically by the hands as they began to pour between decks.

West ran forward with them, caught up in the excitement of a small-scale war. He leapt like a tiger when the moment came, landing with a thud on the maindeck of the other ship. He picked himself up hurriedly.

The clash of steel against steel assaulted his ear from every side, while scattered pistol shots echoed through the smoke of the carronades. There was a copper-skinned face; slash at it—it disappears. Another frightened expression, another savage slash across the throat, a spurt of blood and a feeble yell. Next, he came up against a fellow with a blade of his own, an expression of fierce determination showing on the set jaw below the moustache. No matter. A scrape of sword against sword—nearly had him, there. A lunge. Got part of his shirt, perhaps a little flesh. Fake, block, strike, lunge, block, slash. West was backing up, towards the rail. Mustn't give up ground. Another savage blow, met with a clang instead of a thunk. Blast! Still fighting. Had the other fellow slowly backing away; he was tired out. Slash, block. Dodge that blow—an opening! Lunge, that's it! Got him, right in the chest!

West approached his fallen adversary, the gold-hilted sword protruding grotesquely from his chest. It was an officer; probably a lieutenant. The uniform was now disfigured with a splotch of red, though; the face now frozen in a grimace of final pain. West placed his foot delicately under the poor man's chin, took his sword, and pulled it free with a mighty jerk, feeling the scrape of the blade between his ribs. He grimaced. This was the side of war that he hated intensely. West turned away from the terrible sight, looking toward the maindeck, where some of the hands were still engaged in scattered struggles.

For some moments the Spaniards gave way, as though terrified, and backed into the waist. But there they rallied; now there was desperate fighting, hard, cruel blows dealt and received. For a moment, it seemed that the enemy would triumph, but then someone from *Perseverance*'s crew hauled down the Spanish ensign. The colors had been struck. It was over.

Slowly, the fighting ebbed all around West, as his crew made prisoners of their Spanish counterparts. He paused, and looked down at himself. He must pose quite a spectacle, he thought, with his blood-spattered white breeches, torn uniform jacket, crooked hat, and gory sword. He removed a handkerchief from his right sleeve and wiped clean his newly-proven blade. It would serve him well, he said to himself, as he looked down on it.

"Cap'n, sir?" West looked up, startled out of his daydreaming by a rugged-looking hand with his dagger in the back of a Spanish officer with a proud yet subdued, wilted expression. He wore a moustache, but it was better trimmed than the other fellow he'd battled. On his breast, he bore the Legion of Honor; that was a French medal, established by Bonaparte himself, the dog. This Spaniard must've stolen it off of the corpse of a frog on some battlefield. Barbarian. Feeding even from his allies. Not all Spanish were so disgustingly uncivilized, but here was a prime example.

"Me llamo Marcos Felipe Alejandro de Sabanta, del *Valiente.*" He stated in his native language, introducing himself as captain of the *Valiente*, or, roughly translated, the "Courageous". West himself spoke a little Spanish; he'd been combating privateers in Central America as a midshipman years ago. The other captain proffered his hefty saber.

"I accept your surrender," West said in Spanish. "and I congratulate your officers and men at a battle hard-fought. Please accept the hospitable quartering and decks of my ship, U.S.S. *Perseverance*, twenty-two guns. Would you care for tea? Coffee?"

"No." de Sabanta replied simply, glaring down his nose at West. He must be in total disgrace for losing such a fine frigate to a mere sloop.

"I accept your surrender, then, and ask you to gather your officers—unarmed, mind you—on the quarterdeck. You will be transferred to the *Perseverance*." He took the man's sword. They exchanged salutes, and all were soon ready to be taken prisoner.

He surveyed the enemy's deck. *Valiente* was a big sprawling frigate, very obviously of Spanish design and construction. Aside from a new mainmast and perhaps some patchwork for her copper, she was in relatively good shape. A pretty figure in prize money, thought West to himself, for he and the crew. No other vessels in sight, so his was the lone recipient. Once the Privateer Squadron was reached, each ship could contribute men to her skeleton crew, a jury mainmast rigged, and prisoners transferred. Commodore Estleman would undoubtedly enjoy the prospect of another ship under his unhindered authority; any man would. West had been a commander for slightly more than a week, and already he was making a name for himself.

"Mr. Caswell!" he called suddenly. His location relative to the mast had changed; he'd been pacing without realizing it.

"Yes, sir?" There was the second lieutenant, looking battered and bloody, but still with a smile on his face.

"Choose a prize crew for yourself. I am appointing you as prizemaster of this frigate, and I trust she'll be in good hands. Use the Spaniards for labor as much as you wish; I want that wreckage cut away and a jury mainmast in place by an hour before dawn," he spat. "See that the Spanish surgeon attends to his wounded in the cockpit, but see if you can confine the other prisoners to the maindeck as much as possible. I want both quarterdeck and all four fo'c'stle carronades aimed inward at them; double loads of grape shot should suffice. Keep a coil of match lit constantly. Triple watch shifts, deck patrols, marine guard. Do you understand?"

"Aye aye, sir."

"I should hope so. Mr. Tallis!"

"Sir?"

"Call away my gig. I want to be back aboard in five minutes. Have the surgeon set to work on our wounded immediately." West was filled with real concern for his men, and prayed inwardly that casualties had been light.

"Of course, sir."

"The correct response is 'aye aye,' I believe."

"Aye aye, sir."

Somehow, all of that had felt very satisfying. Firing off order after order decisively had a special reserved pleasure to it, one that could only be felt by a naval captain at sea. Abuse of power was one thing; rapid and effective commanding was quite different.

When he turned around to descend the side to his gig, (the unanchored *Valiente* had drifted during the course of the battle), he was shocked at the expressions meeting his glance. Some of the crewmen were smiling; some stone-lipped, but all looked upon him with what could only be described, he realized, as sheer admiration. Even the officers seemed as awed by him. *Admiration*. He realized, with a start, that they liked him. He'd been harsh, downright unruly, and often curt, and yet somehow they respected him for it. The men looked upon him as a hero, the officers as a future Nelson; he knew he was neither. How ridiculous! He, Lowell West, a naval genius? It was absurd. He felt suddenly irritated; he was at a loss to explain why, though.

There was still so much to be done, as well. The capture was made, but the battle had not ended. As he descended to his gig, he thought of the long night that awaited him; repairs to be made, prisoners to be interviewed, and wounded to be tended. It would be a long while before he slept.

A sigh put it all out of his mind. He'd won, he'd come out on top. A sloop had beaten a frigate! And all with an inexperienced captain, an old ship, and an undrilled crew.

CHAPTER 5

"Mr. Tallis, get her royals in!" West shouted, straining to be heard over the howl of the wind. A squall had blown up just after midnight, calling him from his bed and making work on the *Valiente*'s mainmast much more difficult. It was finished now; Caswell was to be commended for that.

Now *Perseverance* was heaving and lee-lurching quite unpredictably as she lay over to the wind. In her current battered, lead-filled form, the strain on her ribbing was immense. He thought of ordering men to the rudder cables, but soon dismissed the idea as unnecessary. The wind increased in force quite suddenly, though, calling another mournful note to West's ears as it harped through the rigging.

West stood on the ship's starboard side, leaning heavily against the quarterdeck rail in a struggle to remain on his feet in the pounding rain. Beneath him, the deck corkscrewed as her bows plunged in the trough of a great Atlantic roller. Ah, here was Tallis, looking nearly as green as the Spanish sea.

"I'll have the t'gallants off her, Mr. Tallis!" he called, as the wind increased still further. Evidently, the first lieutenant answered with the customary "Aye aye, sir," because West saw him form the words with his mouth, but the sound was drowned out entirely by the roar of the unrelenting squall. The ship gave a sudden, sickening lurch as she was hit dead on the port beam by a powerful, sweeping wave. As he fought to keep his balance, Tallis once again loomed up out of the blowing darkness beside him.

"Wind's coming in broad on the port quarter, sir!" he shouted to the captain. Still, he was barely heard. Each man pulled his boat cloak tighter about him as the fierce storm raged.

"Thank you, Mr. Tallis!" The first lieutenant knuckled his forehead and disappeared once more. It would be necessary to trim sail still more severely.

"Haul that sheet in!" he called over the fury of the storm. Above him, the topmen were still grappling with the topgallants, trying to furl them before they could be torn off. To lose spars or sails now would be unacceptable; it was highly probable that, during the day's battle, the spares with the carpenter's stores had been damaged beyond use or recognition.

He couldn't imagine the agonies endured in the cockpit right now. There were wounded men for whom the scalpel could not wait; the surgeon would have to operate to the best of his ability in almost total darkness, with the unsteady heave and pull of the ship combating his practiced hand. Even now, over the wild creaking of the ship and the screaming gale, he thought he could hear wails from below-deck.

Parts of the rail were missing, ropes in the rigging had been snapped, and sails were scarred by shot. Below water, shot holes let the sea into the bilge with every plunge. The clank of the pumps leapt to the ear at the moment, like a steady bass drum keeping time to the orchestral singing of the storm.

God, she moving sluggishly, thought West. The ship was waterlogged and heavy with the ocean she'd taken on, and forty men were at the pumps at this very moment. Still she was sinking under his very feet. West was about to order all idle hands to the pumps when he heard a hail from the foremast watch.

"Deck there! Sail on the horizon!" came the yell. Instantly, West had a glass to his eye.

Through the blowing darkness off the starboard bow could be seen the double pinpricks of the stern lights of a ship of war. At this distance, the two lanterns seemed to meld into one.

"I'm going up," he said instantly, though he was sure no one heard him. Striding quickly, he picked his way to the mizzen shrouds and began to inch upward. In several places, ropes were missing, so the climb took him several minutes. A hundred feet below, the deck swam in sickening circles as he tried, in vain, to steady himself on the masthead. Glass to his eye.

The first dim rays of sunlight were now beginning to crawl up over the horizon, or he would not have been able to see anything at all. There was certainly a ship there, though; a heavy frigate. She looked almost British or French, but, by her low outline, he could tell that she was neither. The cut of her sails wasn't British either. She could well be American.

And then, as he watched, a dim blur next to the distant vessel solidified into a second ship—smaller certainly, but nearly as powerful. Another appeared, and soon another, and West's heart leapt. The Privateer Squadron! There they were, they had to be, perhaps six hours sailing in the storm. The sun might rise to quell the wind a little, it was true, but they were in sight at any rate.

By the time West had set foot on deck again, the brilliant red Spanish sun was pulling itself free of the horizon. The squall was letting up now, edging off, little by little. *Perseverance* was able to set her topgallants again, and royals soon followed. She heeled over much less, running fast for the other American ships.

West, having fought a hard battle the previous day and remaining on deck for most of the night, was thoroughly exhausted. His legs burned from overuse, his eyes felt gummy and sore, and both his arms tingled numbly. As he hooked his elbow into the hammock shrouds for support, he could just see up over the lofty poop. Two cable's lengths astern of his ship, he could barely make out the *Valiente*, with her jury mainmast, following *Perseverance*'s tack as he had ordered. After looking her over for assurance that her prize crew hadn't been evicted by angry prisoners, West turned back to face his own maindeck and forecastle.

"Mr. Tallis!" he called, that old quarterdeck rasp of his coming at his command, lively as ever. When Tallis answered, the concerned look on his face revealed to the captain exactly how tired he looked to his crew.

"Yes, sir?"

"Pass the word for Mr. Louis and the ship's carpenter."

"Aye aye, sir." The call was taken up down the length of the ship.

West, with a last once-over of his injured sloop, turned on his heel and proceeded, throbbing lower half notwithstanding, down the companion to the aft cabin. Slowly, he peeled off the sou'wester and pilot's jacket, laying them across the breach of a stern-chaser to dry. Checking to be sure that he was dry, (if he got his little cot wet in any capacity, it might never be fully restored), he lay his tired self upon it with a satisfied sigh. He was nearly asleep when there was a prim little knock on the door. With a groan of resentment at having sent for anyone at this state of exhaustion, he rose and went to his desk chair.

"Come in," he said, sounding fully awake.

Ah. Here was Louis, the ship's surgeon, evidently fresh from the horrors of the cockpit. He presented quite a spectacle at opening the door, his apron and the shirt beneath it soaked through with human blood. His sweat-streaked face was not pleasant, though his hands had evidently been recently washed in seawater; they were clean. When his captain beckoned, he did not sit down, owing to the bodily fluids that covered him.

"You summoned me, sir?" he coughed, his voice grating in its usual, deep rasp.

"Yes, Mr. Louis. I would like a complete report on our losses."

"It's hard to say exactly how many dead, sir; that number could be changing every moment. Right now, though, it would seem that we have seven dead, with four that won't last another hour. Total casualties number thirty-eight."

He winced at the number. It would never be easy for him to alleviate the guilty feeling associated with the loss of men under his command. All the same, that was surprisingly good after the pounding they had earlier received. West next posed a question as to the general nature of the wounds.

"Well, sir," Louis replied, furrowing his brows. "We've got at least four that aren't going to make it, like I said. Maybe more than that. Most of the injuries are pretty mild, though; treatable. Wooden splinters less than two feet long. Burns by powder, searings by cannonballs. Some grape shot buried in an arm or leg. Survivable; they'll be to work again in a week or two, some without all their limbs, but all the same, alive.

"Thank you, Mr. Louis." West was happy about that, at least. Later on today, the bodies of the seven (or possibly eleven) dead would be sent overside; a short ceremony, most likely. Only seven so far, with four more possible! The surgeon had certainly done an excellent job.

Louis touched his forehead and bowed out, returning, presumably, to the humid hell that awaited him below.

As he shut the door, there was a second flourishing of knocks upon it almost immediately. Apparently, the ship's carpenter had been waiting just outside during the interview. West bade him enter, and, when told to be seated, he complied.

Burns was a short, stocky fellow with a build typical to that of a long-time seaman. He spoke with a twinge of a Scottish accent, and always seemed to be staring straight past you with his heavy grey eyes.

"Ya wanted ta' see me, sir?" he said, looking perfectly at ease in his captain's cabin, a place where few of his peers would ever have the honor of sitting.

"Good day, Mr. Burns," West smiled at him. Burns expressed a similar sentiment. "I trust you have made a full inspection of the vessel's overall damage?"

"I heve, sir," he replied, with a grim smile. "We've got eleven major shot-holes in err side, six of whech err below the copper, in her hull. I heve been below thar, sir, and heve seen th' damage with me own eyes. Tisn't pretta, I'm afraid. Bilge is nigh on five feet, I'd say, with twenty men a' the poomps night 'n day. The main an' quarterdeck have been repeatedly blasted with shot as well, an' as ya know, sir," he said, stealing a glance round the splintered walls of West's own cabin. "The holds an' cabins, including yarr own an' the wardroom, err in need of some patchin'. New standing an' running rigging will be needed in several places, an'—though tisn't me place, sir—ya'd better git the sailmaker ta work on them canvas!"

West sighed in frustration. It would take some considerable time to restore *Perseverance* to her previous operating condition. Repairs would have to be started at once; hopefully, they could all be completed at sea.

"What is your recommendation on a course of action?"

"Well, sir, it's hard to say, really. I can git a sail up under her hull ta plug up most o' the shot-holes, but that won't do it all. Eventually, she'll heve ta be beached fer complete repairs. All the rest can be done pretta quick-like, sir, I'd think."

"Can you finish most of it—quality work, mind you—before we join the squadron?"

"How long's that?"

"Five hours."

Burns exhaled sharply, turning it into a whistle near the end. A look of intense concentration came into his face.

"I think so, sir, if I git a move on it. Shall I tell tha sailmaker to git started as well?"

"If you would be so kind…?"

"Certainly, sir."

West sat still for a moment, lips pursed, hands folded. The sail, he supposed, would suffice for the time being, and the rest of Burns' repairs could probably serve permanently. They would most likely have to wait until their return to the States to get her hull-up on a beach, though; if islands existed in the Biscay region with the proper type of coast, it could well be done there, but it was doubtful. He would have to keep men at the pumps constantly. Even then, they might not make headway on the water, torrents of which were rushing in at the very moment. He sighed again, and leaned forward over his desk. She was sinking under his very feet, he knew. Immediate countermeasures were required.

"Thank you, Mr. Burns. Begin all necessary repairs immediately."

"Of course, sir."

"That will be all."

"Aye aye, sir." Burns said, knuckling his forehead as he ducked out of the cabin.

West glanced at the numerous shot-holes in the starboard wall of his cabin. Through them, he could see a thin mist rising off the grey ocean in the early morning light. He was exhausted; that he knew only too well. But it was time to go on deck.

West appeared on the quarterdeck, at his usual place (just aft of the helm), only a few minutes later. He was wearing his boat-cloak and gloves along with his dirty white breeches and cocked hat; the squall had dissipated to a light, annoying drizzle. His sou'wester and pilot's jacket were now unnecessary. It was a gloomy morning, though; the sky shrouded in an impenetrable layer of clouds, the sun hidden beneath a similar veil. The rain that was blown occasionally into his face was just that; rain, with no scattered spray mixed with it. Somewhere in the distance, thunder rolled lazily across the sky. The seas were still choppy and windblown, with water creaming up under the bows as *Perseverance* plunged steadily onward to make her distant rendezvous. The sails of the largest of the other American ships were only just visible from deck now, stars and stripes flapping contentedly from her mizzen yard.

Astern, *Valiente* was making her own slow progress through the waves, moving rather quickly for her present condition. Not near *Perseverance*'s steady seven knots, though. It was to be expected.

West, having made the usual survey of his decks, set to pacing starboard and port behind the helm. There was a long wait to be had before he joined the squadron, and he knew he could not sleep that entire time. For once, he had actual time to think. All scuttled fearfully out of the captain's way when the black look on his face was noted by the junior lieutenant. Around him, sails were mended, the railing was patched, and preventive tackles and braces repaired. He noticed none of it.

Inside him, there was a sudden and deep need to think for awhile, and think he did. A struggle took place there—one that arose so quickly he had not the time to fight it down. What ensued was unexplainable; a rapid string of thoughts and realizations that none could have been prepared for. His thoughts were in Massachusetts; his mother, their little home by the harbor; England. Spithead. The Thames River, Smallbridge, Tor Bay, London. The home of his birth, about which he remembered so little, but for which he was so proud. Of his father, that old craggy face, the rough hands that came from a life at sea. Gunfire; somewhere he remembered it. Must be the Revolution. Patriotism. Here he paused, and a slow feeling of—what was it? It was hard to identify. It felt as though the entire mechanism that *was* his very self had been wrenched up out of the depths of his soul for inspection, and found to be horribly incomplete. There was something missing, something that had been lost somewhere in an earlier line of thought. He sensed this, and it gave him pause to continue—but he also sensed the need for uncovering the feelings that had lain dormant for all the many years he'd lived. Something was wrong; he could not put his finger on it precisely, but there was something about his identity that had to be thought through, and thought through this instant. It was very odd; something that had never been felt before; why now was beyond him entirely. And yet—

He loved the country that he served here at sea, the country that his father had so believed in. He felt a calling to the United States, a sense of belonging there, and yet he yearned to see Britain for the sake of his heritage. How was it possible to feel loyal to both countries, when they were so far separated? Reason for such conflict was unknown. He felt suddenly empty, incomplete, dissatisfied; he realized with horror that he'd somehow felt that way all his life. He believed in the country whose flag he flew enough to die for it; that he knew wholeheartedly. And yet—somehow he remained unfulfilled until he could be acknowledged for what he truly was, an Englishman, but an American all the same. In all of his inward turmoil, West did not notice the squadron looming nearer and nearer—until, abruptly, he looked across *Perseverance*'s bows, and there it was. And suddenly he knew that he wasn't alone in his confusion, that there was another who shared his plight, and must have dealt with it similarly in his time. James Estleman—the commodore to whose command he was about to submit.

Estleman had established quite a reputation for himself in the American fleet, called by many the Nelson of his country. And yet he was not an American. During the Revolution, he had served as a lieutenant aboard a British ship of the line, but had defected to the American side early in the war. Why, no one quite knew—perhaps for the same unexplainable reasons that made West's own father and so many others like him seek out this new world of intrigue and principles. It was he, Estleman, that had exerted such a powerful influence over John Adams and the whole of Congress to establish a navy after the war, and had been promptly appointed Rear Commodore. He exerted such an influence over the War Department that he planned his own assignments, hand-picking the captains under him in most cases. Why West had been chosen by him, he could only speculate at. Old captain Wilson had often spoken of his days serving as first lieutenant on Estleman's ship during and just after the war. There might just be a connection there—but it was unlikely. Things were often done that way in the modern navy, thought West—but it seemed too improbable to have happened in his case. Yes, Estleman, too, must have felt the same conflict—not of interest; loyalty to America was firm and unwavering in both cases—but of heart. What it all meant, West did not know, and probably would never. But that hole, that incomplete feeling—

Perhaps it was just the loneliness of command catching up to him for the first time. No, no. That wasn't all of it. The reason he thought about it just now; perhaps. But not the entire feeling.

Another look up at the approaching squadron made West bring himself out of the fit that he'd worked into. A cold sweat formed on his brow—that was not appropriate, thought he, for a captain in service. It would interfere with his work, this confusion. He must put it all out of his mind; forget it for the remainder of this commission. Banish it; yes, that was the word he was searching for. He must focus only on the things at hand.

"Mr. Sway!" he called suddenly, ceasing that infernal pacing that he'd begun and noticing that the Privateer Squadron was now much closer.

Once captain and personal attendant stood together on the quarterdeck, both proceeded below. There, West began to don his best uniform. Above him on deck, he heard the musical *ting* of the ship's bell, and the watch being called. He wore his best dress-coat for his uniform, gold-hilted cutlass, and gold-laced cocked hat. These he put on slowly, making sure that everything was in order, along with his finest white breeches, least-worn trousers, and pinchbeck-buckled shoes. Finally, he stood before his mirror and parted his hair to perfection. The first impression he made with Estleman was going to be a good one.

As he finished with the uniform, he turned to Sway.

"Pass the word for Mr. Tallis," he said, the earlier mental conflict entirely forgotten. He felt good, despite that empty feeling that had plagued him only moments before. He knew that he would not again be bothered until he was ready to think things out.

"Pass the word for Mr. Tallis!" Sway echoed, and the sentry outside took up the call as well. Soon, the first lieutenant knocked at the door, and was hurriedly beckoned in.

"You wanted to see me, sir?" he said upon arrival. He was wide-eyed with admiration at the sight of his captain's dress uniform.

"Yes, Mr. Tallis. I want all of the hands in their blue and white, not the rags they presently flout before me. Have the drummers prepared to beat, the bos'un's mates at attention for our salute of the flagship. Eleven guns, I believe?"

"Eleven, sir."

"Mm. Inform Mr. Nettleton, if you please, and have them loaded and run out on the double. Quarter charges. Is all of that quite clear, Mr. Tallis?"

"Quite, sir."

"I expect it executed by the time I am on deck…please take the time to notice the stage at which my uniforming progresses. We know that I will make my appearance once my compliment of clothes is complete, do we not?"

"Of course, sir," said Tallis, gulping when he saw that he had only a few moments indeed.

"That will be all then, Mr. Tallis."

"Aye aye, sir."

A salute, a slammed door, and the fellow had disappeared.

West chuckled to himself in the mirror, turning out the cuffs of his shirt in an attempt to appear somewhat fashionable before the commodore. He knew that Tallis was unwaveringly faithful and indubitably reliable, so that his orders would be carried out ages before he went above deck. With a last smirk at his reflection—he always appeared slightly ridiculous decked out in full regalia—he straightened his sword, slammed the cocked hat on his head, and flung open his cabin door.

When *Perseverance*'s captain appeared on her quarterdeck, Nettleton was in the waist awaiting the order to set off the guns, and the hands stood at impeccable fall-in. He gave the ship a rapid once-over. There was now no visible evidence that any battle had taken place; Burns had worked hard, fast, and well. The railings were intact, the deck no longer splintered. Aloft, all of the damaged rigging had been replaced (standing and running), and the sails were patched once again. Now it was only the damage below waterline that had to be repaired; a sail would be up under the hull the following day, and the various damaged bulkheads and hammocks in the 'tween decks would be fixed.

Below, the steady metallic clanking of the pumps had not ceased; even when the captain was about to make his inspection, they had to be manned. No headway could be lost on that infernal seawater.

Perseverance's deck had been swabbed to a shimmering white, and now lay un-cluttered and entirely spotless. Lined up along the starboard bow were the bodies of the dead; nine at the moment, perhaps another two to join them. Each corpse was sewn into its own white canvas hammock with a twelve-pound ball at the feet. They would all be committed to the sea later that afternoon. As West looked round his deck, he could not help but notice the dark outline of the Privateer Squadron looming ever closer off the port bow. All he had to do was set the royals, order a shallow turn to port, perhaps one point. Perhaps two, and they would join them within half an hour.

West next turned his eyes on his crew. They looked perfectly uniform with their straw boaters (with navy-blue bands), white trousers, navy-blue shirts and bordered white neckerchiefs. The captain looked on them with pride; these men *were* the navy. They had all made him proud in the past, and he had no doubt that they'd never fail him in the action to come. He found it amazing, the blind trust with which they followed him. Not a single one of them had the slightest idea that an incredible danger awaited them; the danger of an undeclared war. They were fine men, no doubt about it, and they could perform twice as well as they looked.

"All hands aloft to loose the sails!" West suddenly yelled, transforming immediately the two thin double-lines of crewmen into a swarm of scattered hands, running this way and that to their stations high above deck in the rigging. The spiders scurried upward once again, spinning webs to catch the wind.

"Set royals full!" West was now hollering, vaguely hearing his lieutenants echoing him and moving forward to enforce the order. "Mr. Foster, two points a-port!"

"Two points, sir."

"Take one reef out of the fore tops'l! Mr. Nettleton, get for'rard to take charge of your guns!"

"Aye aye, sir!"

Already, the ship was gathering headway, despite the torrents of water in her draft, and running hard for her allies.

For only a few minutes more, *Perseverance* maintained that tack, changing abruptly as she was about to join the squadron. As she pulled in, the flagship fired a gun in greeting, and West ordered Nettleton's salute in consequence. It appeared that there were a total of four ships in the squadron; five with *Perseverance* as well. Two sloops, a brig, a frigate, and then—

West stifled a gasp as he looked at the flagship for the first time. She was not only brand-new, completed only a year before, but was one of the stars of the American navy. It was the U.S.S. *United States*, forty-four guns, and sister ship to the *Constitution*. She was immense and powerful, yet quick and well-handling. Scoffed at first and then highly praised, it was rumored that any ship of her design could out-run, out-fight, or out-maneuver any other vessel afloat. It was every American captain's dream to serve aboard one of *Constitution's* sisters; *Constellation*, *United States*, or *President*. This Estleman must be a truly great leader indeed to gain command of such a jewel. She was beautiful beyond any imagination.

"Flagship signaling, sir!" called Tallis excitedly from the main-deck, unnecessarily. Even West could see the flags leaping up her signal halyard. The signaling midshipman stepped forward, his face calm, his glass ready. He raised it, and, after a moment's pause—

"It's our number, sir!" he pulled his eye briefly away, and then began to translate:

"Flag to *Perseverance*; delighted to see you. To captain; will you dine with me at four bells?" that was in only a few minutes; West would have to hurry.

"Reply to the affirmative, Mr. Tallis."

"Aye aye, sir."

He paused, looked about the deck, and saw that every eye was on him. His ship had officially joined the squadron, rumors of sealed orders were circulating throughout the ship's company, and he had just been invited to dine with perhaps the greatest naval genius in the American nation.

"Mr. Tallis!" he called.

"Yes, sir?"

"Call away my gig."

"Aye aye, sir."

The hands, who had been milling about on the maindeck in a disorderly fashion, were dispersed to carry out the order. The coxswain and his mates readied the little boat for launch as West gave the first lieutenant his remaining orders.

"Take charge of the ship, Mr. Tallis. The hands may remove their uniforms, but keep them looking sharp for the Commodore. Post the signal midshipman, of course, and raise a flag if anything should happen out of the ordinary."

"Aye aye, sir," he said, touching his hat. West returned the compliment, and began to descend the side, to the wild twittering of the boatswain's pipes.

Delicately, he arranged himself in the sternsheets of his gig, just remembering to order his coxswain to "Pull away." Ahead lay the sprawling *United States*, gargantuan in comparison to the tiny sloop of his command. Her glorious gundecks, ports closed at the moment, loomed up before the little rowboat, reminding him again of the inferiority of his own vessel. Finally the two craft were side by side, and West ascended the boarding netting of the large ship.

Whistles twittered as his head appeared at deck level, and the rest of him soon followed. The flag lieutenant stepped forward with a salute to greet him.

"Commander West?"

"It is I."

"Welcome aboard the U.S.S. *United States*, flagship of the Privateer Squadron. The Commodore awaits your company in his aft cabin, sir."

"Thank you," West said simply, striding to the door of the cabin at the lieutenant's gesture. There he paused, taking a deep breath. He surveyed himself carefully. He, though junior to all of the other post-captains in the squadron, posed quite a picture in his full uniform. Making an attempt at a feeble smile, he breathed deeply once more, steadied his left hand casually on the hilt of his cutlass, and flung wide the door.

The huge stern windows caught the eye immediately; they let in an unimaginable amount of sunlight, despite the cloudy sky. Next, it became apparent just how pitiful West's own cabin was in comparison.

Where West had simple canvas curtains, Estleman had the finest silk; there were upholstered chairs and firm pillows to match. In the center of the space was a large, ornately carved old table, presumably nailed to the deck. And the deck, the deck!

There was an oriental rug that covered most of the exposed wood beneath his feet. None of this could ever be furnished by the American Navy itself; it was an institution just barely able to scrape by with normal expenses. Estleman must be a very rich fellow.

Aside from the room, of course, there was the man himself. When West entered, Rear Commodore James Estleman had been leaning against the sill of one of the huge windows, gazing out at the ship's wake. Now, though, he had turned around and given a smile at the sight of his new guest.

He was short; most geniuses were, it seemed. Augustus had been short. Napoleon was short. Perched precariously on the top of Estleman's head was a heavily powdered white wig, and his little body seemed to match precisely. The big blue uniform appeared heavy with gold; along with the lace, countless medals and awards (many of them British), were pinned to his left breast. The shoes were of fine black leather with gilt buckles, the stockings of glorious silk, and the breeches of unbroken white. His face, a kindly but eccentric one, bore a long scar down one cheek. He seemed quite a fellow; West liked him at once.

"Ah," he said, speaking in a soft but dignified voice. "Commander West! It is wonderful to meet you at long last." He extended a beefy hand; West shook it politely. "I have heard quite a lot about you from an old friend, Captain Wilson, formerly of the *Nova*. I hear you have made an excellent impression on him, commander. Indeed I hope so; the assignment I have for you requires a man of skill!"

That was it. All of this—his promotion, his command, his posting in Spain—all of it was Wilson; Estleman was putting an immense amount of trust in judgment in his friend.

"Yes, sir," West replied lamely, thinking of nothing better to say. He stepped forward to the huge table and, at the commodore's gesture, took his seat.

Estleman was twisted around in his chair, just opposite West, apparently looking out the window again. After a moment, he turned, giving the young commander a piercing stare that startled him. A wry smile quickly followed.

"If you don't mind my query, Captain," he paused, leaning forward slightly as though with interest. "How the devil did you acquire that frigate? Illegal business dealings, I suppose? Haw! Don't look at me that way, my dear sir, I merely tease, I merely tease. But truthfully now, by what device did it enter your hands?"

"Well, sir, I captured it."

"Captured it? In a battle?"

"Yes, sir."

"With resistance?"

"Indeed."

"Your sloop wasn't sunk to St. Rose?"

"No, sir."

"Good God!" Estleman sat back with astonishment, a smile splitting his face. "Details, my boy, details! Your verbal report!"

West related the entire episode, from the sighting of the enemy to her full capture and prize assignment. At the end of the tale, which West tried to keep short and to the point, though it soon became something of a novel, Estleman sat back with a look of approval implanted upon his visage.

"Very impressive, my good sir, for a sloop of twenty-two to capture a frigate of such size. Very impressive indeed; I shall mention this most favorably in my report to the War Department. Ah! Our dinner is here." A taller man, presumably the commodore's attendant, entered, bearing two covered silver platters issuing steam from their edges. No words passed between the commander and the commodore as the food was uncovered, and each began to eat.

The meal was exquisite. Fresh roast lamb, perfectly seasoned and very tender, tossed green salad with a dressing West had never had before, beef stew, and, as a grand finale, treacle tarts. West ate like a starved man, gulping down his wine—which seemed the best he'd ever tasted—and food in only a few moments. With a contented sigh he leaned back into the cushioned chair, wiping his lips lightly with the corner of a napkin. If only the navy could spare such ingredients and such cooking talent on a mere post-captain, West felt as though the months spent sleeping on a hard straw mattress and days wandering about in clothes that were always slightly damp could be bearable.

The gracious host finished not long afterward, leaning back in a similar manner with the same satisfied sigh. Apparently, Estleman recognized the desirability of a small period devoted to digestion after supper, and so he beckoned the young commander into another comfortable chair at his desk and took the seat opposite him. The conversation that followed carried a much different tone than before. Business was in the air.

"I am acting on my friend's advice at your appointment here; I had no knowledge of an officer suitable for the task I have ahead, and so I turned to my friend for his recommendation. It follows that an equally suitable vessel was found, and you were given command; here you are now. It is obvious by Captain Wilson's reports of you that you are highly thought of by former commanding officers. I hope I will find such a pleasure in the present situation." The commodore sighed. "I also hope that I am not making a mistake. You see, Commander, the assignment I have in store for you is one that few would care to undertake; a struggle against the odds in a war that shouldn't be happening, with a small chance of victory and not much glory. Indeed, if your actions are widely known, Tripoli will be joined by Spain and France against us. We cannot afford that; at all costs, this must be kept relatively quiet."

"I understand fully, sir," West replied, chilled suddenly at what he was about to be sent to do, but eager nonetheless. Estleman sighed again. He was obviously about to reach the point.

"There is a place, Commander, down the Spanish coast before the Portuguese border, a river's mouth into the Atlantic. Ria de Arosa, as it's known. The waterway is a small one—river is quite an odd title—and filled with small islands and sudden shoals. Fully store-laden frigates or anything larger are impossible to pass—that is by design. But a little brig or a sloop would be perfectly safe. At the source of this waterway, which is not far upstream, there lies a shipyards, and the one that is solely devoted to the construction and repair of naval craft patrolling the English Channel, the northern Atlantic, and the Bay of Biscay. If this shipyards could be disabled or destroyed, it would be a great blow to the Spanish, hindering their naval force for perhaps years. This would solve our problem, and, perhaps more importantly, make it possible for the British to defeat the French and Spanish in a naval action, once and for all."

"It will be my job to destroy this shipyards," said West plainly. The commodore smiled.

"Unfortunately, it is not quite as simple as that. You see, the shipyards is, as I have said, surrounded by an intricate network of islands and shoals. On the little inlet itself, the left side is clear of these obstructions, though still very shallow. It is this side of the channel that all of the newly-launched vessels use as a thoroughfare, to leave the river and sail north for supplies. Since these ships aren't yet loaded, their draft is reduced, and they can make it through hull-up. But because of this, their fighting capacity is greatly hindered, so that any patrolling vessel—such as your own—would find them easy prey to attack. To this fact, the obvious helplessness of the craft, we owe the fortress and shore battery at Santa Eugenia, a city situated high at the top of a cliff on the clear side of the channel. They will not find it difficult to sink you, should cause be given. Flaunting the Stars and Stripes along the coast is cause enough for them, I might add. The difficulty is in *entering* the Ria de Arousa; once inside, all ships and shore sites become, as I said, easy prey. It's up to you to enter safely, hide amongst the islands, ambush, capture and sink as many supply vessels (bound for the shipyards) and warships as you can, destroy the shipyards themselves, and get safely out again. The fortress will have to be dealt with as you see fit; just take some measure to ensure that you won't be sunk on sight. Those forty-two pounders'll do it. Got all that, my boy?"

West paused a moment before answering.

"Yes, sir."

"Very good," said Estleman, rising to his feet. The interview was at an end. "You'll receive your full written orders at dawn; see that you set sail not long after. It was a pleasure to make your acquaintence, sir, I am sorry that your duty takes you away so soon."

"Thank you for the dinner invitation, sir."

"You're welcome, my boy. Very welcome. Ah! I nearly forgot. You may reclaim your prize crew from that Spanish ship now; you'll need all the manpower you can get. This ship's marine compliment will be detailed to you as well."

"Thank you, sir."

"The best of luck to you, Commander," he was now walking to the door. He opened it; the soft night air and a full sky of stars awaited him outside.

"Good night, sir."

"Good night."

On deck again, West's gig was signaled for, and the sideboys manned the rail. The boatswain and his mates pealed hard on their whistles as he went over the side, but he did not pay any attention. Nor did he again note the incredible vastness of the *United States* as he absent-mindedly ordered his coxswain to "Pull away." He was already planning, his tired mind racing from one idea to the next with incredible rapidity. The full implications of this new set of orders had not yet sunk in; all West felt was numbness. Above him, the stars were dazzling in their beauty, as diamonds set in the infinite blackness of this strange Spanish sky.

"Boat ahoy!"

"*Perseverance!*"

The whistles twittered madly once again as West pulled himself on deck of his own sloop, with Tallis waiting there for any orders he might have. There was no need to mention the early departure the next morning; but there was one thing.

"Mr. Tallis."

"Sir?"

"Send a boat to the *Valiente*; her prize crew may return aboard tonight. And let the marines know that they will have to sleep in shifts for an undetermined amount of time, starting tomorrow." All of the marines stationed aboard *United States* would be joining him in the morning, after all. A little warning on that point, however vague, would be enough.

"Aye aye, sir."

"Thank you Mr. Tallis. You may dismiss the men." The first lieutenant knuckled his forehead, and the captain did the same. Then it was off to work for one, and off to bed for the other.

West sighed as he undressed, Sway nearby to take his clothes from him. The next few weeks would see him pacing his quarterdeck at noon and at midnight, by daylight and darkness; perhaps he would be dead in a week, victim of some stray cannonball or a lucky musket shot. Perhaps he would lose the ship to the shore batteries; perhaps the shipyards would not be totally incapacitated by his efforts. Perhaps, perhaps, perhaps. It was not worth thinking about. All that mattered now was sleep; the sea kept its own timetable, and so must he.

"Anything else, sir?"

"No, Sway. You may retire."

"Thankee, sir, thankee."

West leaned back on his cot, stretching his feet out as far as they would go. Ah! It would be good to sleep. A long day was past, and more like it stretched ahead.

In a moment, he was entirely lost to the world.

CHAPTER 6

"Mr. Caswell's compliments, sir, and the flagship is sending a boat."

"I'll come. My respects to Mr. Caswell."

"Aye aye, sir."

Throwing on his coat and cocked hat, West rushed into the companionway from his cabin. Sway had only just finished serving his breakfast, and it now lay, unattended, at his desk.

Already, half a dozen telescopes were trained on the little dinghy from *Perseverance*'s quarterdeck. The hands had ceased their daily swabbing of the deck, and were now standing at the rail and pointing at the incoming craft, apparently hoping for mail or news.

"Avast, there!" West shouted, dispersing the group instantly.

"It's the mail, sir," Tallis announced, lowering his glass when he detected the captain at his elbow. Caswell mulled about nearby.

"Yes, the mail," said West, trying hard to appear thoroughly disgusted. "And it should not directly interfere with the workings of an American ship of war. Dismiss all idle officers to their duty."

"Aye, sir," Tallis replied, looking rather sheepish. He had grown to like the captain, and felt ashamed at this err in his judgment.

Soon the quarterdeck was clear of excess lieutenants and midshipmen, and West was free to pace its length as he pleased. The mail would undoubtedly bring letters from his mother; it would be good to hear from her again. His orders would also be there, and, upon their receipt, he would set sail for the western coast of Spain. As yet, there was not a soul aboard the *Perseverance* that had the slightest idea of the fresh assignment, save her captain.

"Boat ahoy!" Tallis suddenly hailed from the quarterdeck.

"Mail and orders!" came the shouted reply. Now there was the sound of the dinghy sloshing alongside, and the footfalls of her coxswain as several large sacks of mail were hoisted into the waist. When they were all safely aboard, the man approached West.

"Cap'n, sir?"

"Yes, that's me."

"Orders from the commodore, sir, an' his compliments." He produced a wax-sealed parchment envelope.

"Thank you." A salute was exchanged, and then the dinghy's crew left the ship and shoved off again. Without even breaking the seal on the orders, West slid them into his pocket. As he did so, Tallis approached him.

"Flagship sending another boat, sir, and it looks like she's packed full with marines."

"Thank you, Mr. Tallis." That would be the full compliment detailed to the *United States*, now under his command.

"Boat ahoy!"

"Personnel!" One by one, a hundred and fifty U.S. marines filed aboard, to awkward and confused stares from the officers and hands. They were told to get below, which they did in an orderly fashion, to stow their belongings with *Perseverance*'s own division. West, after seeing the marine sergeant safely down the hatchway, turned to the first lieutenant.

"Mr. Tallis!"

"Yes, sir?"

"Put the ship about immediately, and ready a departing salute, to be fired when we have steadied on the opposite tack."

"Aye aye, sir." Tallis responded, turning to face the hands and bellowing a rapid string of orders. Foster, the quartermaster, began to spin the wheel.

"Signal Midshipman!" West called, as *Perseverance* began to come fully round.

"Yes, sir?" A young face appeared.

"Run this signal up immediately: *Perseverance* to flag; departing squadron and sailing for Santa Eugenia."

"Aye aye, sir." He dashed off again, returning a moment later to say, "Flag acknowledges and wishes us the best of luck, sir."

"Acknowledge." That was that; the gun salute was booming out from the forward signaling carronade now, and his vessel was on her way, thrashing to southward, where her first action on the most recent commission awaited her.

The crew was more excited and fidgety now. Even the officers seemed curious; West fancied that he was the only man aboard who walked with measured stride. He was thrilled at the prospect of action in the near future, though he must always appear stoically calm before the men. The ship was sailing steadily away from the Privateer Squadron now; presumably they would continue to actively protect American shipping while he was given a free reign on detached service. The faint grey smudge on the horizon that marked the coast of Spain was growing wider; it was time to set a specific course.

"Mr. Tallis, your company once again, if you please."

"Of course, sir."

A pause as the first lieutenant came aft from the capstan.

"Yes, sir?"

"Lay in a course for the Ria de Arousa, on the western coast of Spain. Once that is finished, cast the log; I'd like an estimated time of arrival."

"Aye aye, sir." A salute, a click of heels.

West watched the man go, and then turned to pacing the quarter-deck again. He had roughly sketched out a plan of action for the entrance of the waterway; but there were other things to consider. Precautions to be taken against boarders, for instance. Once his intentions were known by the enemy, they would launch a counter-attack with all the rapidity they could muster. He must be entirely ready for any such situation.

And as for the entrance itself—well, his plan for that would have to be put into effect soon enough. While the hands were dining at high noon, West called the sailmaker into his cabin to begin preparations.

"Do you know what the Spanish colors look like, Mr. Hargrave?"

The sailmaker blinked at him.

"That I do, sir, I should say so."

"Sew a flag for me, then—try to get everything exact, mind you."

"What?"

"I said I want you to sew me a passable Spanish flag, is that understood?"

"Yes, sir. I beg your pardon, sir, but may I ask why?"

"No, you may not. Begin work immediately."

"I—er—aye aye, sir." He shuffled out, scratching his head in bewilderment, presumably to search for pigments and clean sailcloth.

That done, the captain had naught to do but wait. He had never been good at waiting, and knew he was all the worse for it now, but he resigned himself to it nonetheless. Eventually, he forced himself to sleep, to ease his straining mind. What a captain with iron nerves, who could nap like a child when action was imminent and a third of his crew might be dead in an hour!

He did not exactly nap; more accurately, he lay very still and pondered, occasionally dozing off for a few minutes, then jerking awake again at the slightest noise. For a few hours he simply stared at the deckbeams over his head, itching to climb the companion and go on deck, if only just for the sake of being there.

Finally, the watch was called on deck. At this new commotion on the poop above him, West moved to the stern windows of his aft cabin to stare out at *Perseverance*'s wake. He thought briefly of his orders, and then drew his watch and checked it. Nearly four o' clock.

Abovedeck, the commotion suddenly ceased; the men had taken their new positions. No sooner had the noise subsided then a fresh one was heard—this time a yell—from the fore masthead at the main crosstrees.

West was up and moving in a flash. Land or sail must have been sighted on the horizon—closer, perhaps, if the previous watch had been ignorant—and he would be required on deck. Now he heard more muffled shouts, and then the soft *clunk* of boot on wood as someone began to descend the short stair to his cabin. He dove immediately to his bed and attempted to make it appear as though he'd just awoken. He bade the man enter.

"Land sighted two points off the port bow, sir," It was Moore, the eldest of the midshipman, and still a lad by anyone's standards.

"I'll come." West said as calmly as possible, as he draped his coat about his shoulders and donned his hat. Moore saluted and bowed himself out, shutting the door behind him.

Tallis awaited West on the quarterdeck, leaning stiffly against the rail and straightening to attention at the sight of his superior.

"Coast of Spain in sight, sir, seven miles a-lee."

"Port your helm," the captain called to the quartermaster, raising a glass to his eye. There it was, the mouth of the Ria de Arousa. He had made perfect landfall on the coast of Spain.

"By the casting of the log, sir, if we remain on this tack, I daresay we'll weather the coast well before dark." Tallis said.

"Yes, Mr. Tallis," West replied simply, then, glancing aloft, added, "Make sail. I want our speed as great as the wind allows.

"Aye aye, sir."

Tallis began to bellow orders at the foremast hands. Soon, the little spiders were up in their webs again, spinning their majestic sails from the yardarms. West proudly took in the sigh of his moderately-experienced crew working as a seamless machine.

Perseverance lay well over now, and ran, hull up, for the Ria de Arosa and her newest assignment. She was making a healthy nine knots by the next casting, with all viable sail set but her royals.

Now dead a-bows, the dim outline of land loomed increasingly large in West's field of view. He raised a glass again; there was the river's mouth, wide as five of the late *Nova*'s beam. The right side of the channel seemed, at this remote distance, nearly solid with little islands, while left appeared relatively clear. Set up on a sprawling mountain overlooking that left passage, there was a wall of stone peppered with little openings and breaks—the carronade battery at Santa Eugenia. That peak, "Cristobal" by his nautical charts, provided an ideal vantage point for the protection of the waterway. As the ship edged in towards the fort, West could see that it wasn't quite as small as Estleman's description had made it out to be. At least ten forty-two pound cannons, mounted in stone emplacements, made up the bulk of the harbor's defending force. A brigade of light infantry was probably garrisoned there; the fighting would be rough when *Perseverance*'s crew had to storm her walls after the completion of her mission. It suddenly occurred to West that his ship would be nearly visible from shore by now.

"Mr. Tallis!" he called.

"Sir!"

"Pass the word for the sailmaker!"

"Aye aye, sir!"

The cry was taken up round the ship. A moment's silence, and then a familiar beefy form appeared.

"Reporting for duty, sir."

"You have reproduced the enemy's colors?"

"That I have, sir."

"Strike our own, then, and hoist your duplicate."

"Aye aye, sir."

As the proud stars and stripes fell, excited whispers ran through the main body of the crew, gathered on the maindeck. As the Dago flag was run up the halyard, though, an anticipatory hush set in. Good, thought West; he had nearly issued an order for silence, and was grateful that this discipline was unnecessary.

"Mr. Tallis!" West then called, gazing at the Spanish ensign now flying from the mizzen yard.

"Sir?"

"Beat to quarters and clear the deck for action. I'll have the guns loaded and primed but not run out. Send the marine detachment belowdeck as well, if you please." The striking blue uniforms of the two hundred and fifty marines aboard the little sloop would attract undue attention from the Spanish.

To the measured rap of the snare drums, the bulkheads were stricken and the galley fires dropped overside. Powder boys ran up and down the lines, scuttling through the hatch coamings, laden with shot and explosives. There were repeated snaps and cracks as the carronades were loaded, but the roar of the tackles that usually followed never came. The gunports remained closed, the vast weapons stayed inboard.

Perseverance was fast approaching her destination. She was well within range of the batteries now; even so, her captain had to remain on his guard. It was possible that *Perseverance*, as intended, was attracting no unwanted attention, and that all would go as planned in his entrance of the waterway. It was also possible, however, that her true identity had somehow been ascertained, and that the unnerving silence which lay as yet unbroken was meant only to lure him to the base of those cliffs, where he would have no hope of escape from the fury of the guns. Either way, all he could do was remain under sail.

Now the garish Spanish flag could be seen fluttering proudly over the stone battlements as destiny drew ever nearer. They were under the guns now; the angry seas crashed furiously against the nearby foot of the cliff. If her sails were torn to pieces, that was where *Perseverance* would drift, floundering, breaking up, and leaving her survivors to await the cruel torture the Spaniards inevitably had in store. If the ship survived for long enough for the marines to load their weapons, they would have a fighting chance at escaping capture—but could not get away themselves. But, a little to her captain's surprise, the vessel sailed cleanly under the menacing cannons without incident. They were within the sheltering limits of the waterway now, with the shore battery behind them and a mission ahead.

Suddenly, as *Perseverance* fully cleared the Santa Eugenia fort, the gun batteries sprang to life with a series of deafening crashes. Heads whirled about on the quarterdeck; terror-struck and determined eyes focused on the unbelievable. They were trapped, to be sunk for sure!

"Run your guns out along the port side!" Tallis called, though they would be of little use. It would be much more sensible to order the ship about, set full sail, and make a run for it, firing perhaps a single broadside in retreat, but Tallis was not a tactician. West would have corrected the mistake, had he been paying his first lieutenant any attention.

He stood at the poop, glass to the eye, watching the battery closely. There was clearly no hope for his ship; she would be dashed to pieces under the force of those guns and then grounded against the rocky shore, but still her captain searched desperately for a way out. Perhaps a landing party of the marines and his own seamen, to try to affect some damage to the emplacements in a death struggle; but no, that would do little to aid their hopeless situation. The quarterboat and gig, could be cleared and used as vehicles of abandonment for the old sloop; they would be faster and much more difficult targets to sight. It could perhaps be brought about; but neither of these

options seemed correct. There was a chance that any action whatso-
ever would be rendered unnecessary, albeit a small one. If only he
saw what he was looking for...

And there it was. Above the fort, those proud colors lowered a trifle, then restored themselves to their original height. Behind him,
West could hear the preventive tackles roaring outboard in preparation for a broadside. He spun about, seizing a speaking trumpet as
he did so, and trying desperately to make his old quarterdeck rasp
audible over all the shipboard commotion.

"Mr. Tallis! Belay that order immediately—*immediately*, do you
hear me?"

"Aye aye, sir. Belay! Belay!" the bewildered lieutenant screamed.

"Cease all action on the maindeck and lower our colors, count five
seconds, then run them up again, is that understood?"

"Yes, sir!"

"Mr. Nettleton!"

"Sir!"

"Ready the signaling carronade on the port side, and prime it for
nine cannons."

"Aye aye, sir!"

Calmness returned to the deck once more. All understood now;
the Spaniards had recognized him as a Spanish vessel with the customary nine-gun salute, followed by an honorary flag dip. Now, as a
presumably Spanish captain, West had to return the simple compliment, or the Dagoes might start to load their guns with lead as well
as powder.

Tallis, having completed his assigned task, was now furiously pacing the quarterdeck, hiding his face in his jacket to conceal his
humiliation. His captain had virtually proclaimed him a fool before
the ship's company of men; he'd every right to feel ashamed.

West breathed a shaky sigh of relief as the signal gun began to bellow. The situation could well have been disastrous. Had he panicked,
half his ship's compliment might be dead, the other half imprisoned

until who knows when. It would have created a very sticky situation for President Jefferson back home; explaining away an attacking American ship in a foreign port would be very difficult indeed.

Poor Tallis, though, thought West. The man had only done what he thought to be his duty under difficult circumstances, and would now be submitted to every ridicule permitted in the navy, and some that weren't. West approached him, and, seeing the pained face that glanced up at him abruptly, expecting further reprimand, the captain placed a consoling hand on his shoulder. It was a bold gesture, and one virtually unheard of in any navy in the world. Most of his fellow captains wouldn't have given their officers a second thought.

"An unavoidable blunder, Mr. Tallis, and one that will never occur again, I trust," said West, attempting to sound comparatively friendly. He allowed himself a grim smile, gave a salute, and turned away.

Behind him, Tallis watched him go with a look of admiration playing across his face. Here was a man, who, like all captains, seemed aloof, alert, unemotional, and impervious to human discomfort. Yet, at the same time, at a wild contrast to his colleagues, seemed just, understanding, and—should Tallis even dare to think it—kind. He wielded the sword of command boldly, as all officers should, but with it he did not strike down all in his path. This was a unique and rare captain, and one who—Tallis was certain—would go on to become a legend among his men.

In his cabin, West reached under his little cot for a rectangular case; when he found it, he drew out and tuned a violin. He always played before expected action; it was the last purchase he'd made ashore before his new commission, having lost his old instrument in *Nova*'s wreck. He set the fiddle to his shoulder and slowly drew his bow across its strings. Soon, the violin's mournful notes whispered through the ship's timbers, vibrating even the rigging in its tormented beauty. It was the first time his crew had heard him play.

CHAPTER 7

Much to his surprise, West slept soundly that night. His ship had found its anchor among the little islands at the far south side of the channel, where she was out of sight of the prying telescopes at Santa Eugenia.

Now it was dawn, and he'd been pacing his quarterdeck for half an hour already. The usual bustle of shipboard life assailed his ear in the stillness of the early morning; a thin mist enshrouded his vessel as the heave of the Atlantic swell echoed through the bay. Pea coat, pilot's jacket, and woolen gloves had already been removed—now West had doubts about even his uniform coat. It was fast becoming a hot day. The searing Spanish sun was climbing steadily in the eastern sky, now, heating the air around him with a humid thickness he'd never felt before.

West breathed easily as he strode the beam of his ship; overside, the sea rose and fell lazily as it nearly always did. *Perseverance* rode only under her royals, creeping slowly along among the little islands and sudden shoals of the waterway. The casting of the lead was not yet needed; his charts were very clear on depth at this point in the channel.

Something on the peak of one of the nearby hills caught his eye—it appeared to be a darkly-clad figure running along its ridge. Now it was hidden behind the summit of the hill. Had they been

found out? Surely not. The light was as yet too dim for anyone—even with the aid of a spyglass—to see the colors of his uniform at that distance. There it was again, that silhouette of the
person running down the other side of the hill—but now West could
see that it wasn't actually a person at all.

What he'd been glimpsing as a darkly-clad figure had been, in
fact, the highest point of the main topmast of a Spanish merchant
lugger. Now the Spaniard, who had been obscured from view by an
island peak, had come out into the open.

It was a little boat, crew of fifty, at the most, apparently fully laden
with foodstuffs and supplies, bound for the main body of the Spanish fleet, fighting the British with the French off Ushant. A second
figure appeared at the hilltop—another lugger—and then a third
and a fourth. Soon, all were clearly visible, sailing fast for the mouth
of the Ria, entirely unsuspecting as yet. Just then, Tallis spotted them
as well, for he raised a pointing finger in their direction and began to
open his mouth to speak. He was cut off, though, by an order from
his captain.

"Mr. Tallis! Bring the ship about," he called, surveying the deck.
The ship was still cleared for action—he had left it in that condition
overnight, lest trouble arise without warning. The guns were still
loaded, then.

"Aye aye, sir."

"Steady as she goes. Mr. Nettleton!"

"Sir!"

"Take charge of the guns. Do not run them out or open the ports
until I give the order."

"Aye aye, sir!"

The ship heaved her ponderous self about and quickly began to
close on the merchant crafts. Soon, West had the *Perseverance* running hard in their pursuit under full battle sail. He raised a glass to
his eye, surprising himself at the steadiness of his hand.

At this speed, his vessel could easily pass by the other ships without arousing any suspicion (they still flew the Spanish colors, after all). If he were to come hard a-starboard at the end of the pass and strike the false colors, hoist the star-spangled banner, and run his guns out, he would probably be able to cut them off and overwhelm them, still just out of sight of the shore battery. A few shots at each and their colors would come down, and then he could assign prize crews and send them on their way. Simple enough for a first run.

West watched the four luggers as they beat to windward, only barely out of his reach. The thrill of the chase at hand began to quicken his heartbeat. They were past the first vessel now; just barely able to make out the dim forms of the crewmen on its deck. West's own uniform and those of his officers would still be indistinguishable to them. The second fell behind now, and the third.

"Stand to your guns, Mr. Nettleton!" He was about to affect four captures for the United States, the first of many in a war that wasn't official. "Don't give us away as yet!"

"Aye aye, sir!"

The last lugger was drawing nearer; soon they would be alongside her. West would have to wait until *Perseverance* was about half a cable's length beyond her before he ran his guns out. Too soon, and the rest might be able to escape.

Ever closer, ever closer…the bows of the two ships were equal, *Perseverance* drawing ahead. But suddenly–

"Run the guns out along the starboard side! Fire at will! Fire at will!"

West spun on his heel, erupting into a cold fury. Nettleton had given them all away! The guns were outboard now, the carronades loaded—and suddenly a ragged broadside crashed out from the little sloop. The Spanish were panicking aboard the other ship, the crews of the other three luggers struggling now to evade this unseen threat.

"Damn your eyes!" West shouted at Nettleton, and then, still in a rage, "Mr. Tallis, run the American colors up the halyard. If another shot is fired before that's done, we'll have broken the bloody Articles of War. The next man who fires his carronade, I'll shoot with my own hand!"

The Spanish ensign screamed down the mizzen halyard, and the stars and stripes raced to the yard again afterwards. West examined the situation that Nettleton had forced him into.

The Spaniard that had been fired on had already dropped her colors and furled all sail, but the other three were making off in different directions to attempt to escape the American sloop. Bloody hell, thought West. He'd have to hunt them down.

"Mr. Foster, seven points a-starboard! Set royals and drop two reefs of the fore stays'l! Mr. Caswell!"

"Sir!"

"Kindly relieve Mr. Nettleton of his position at the guns! Fire as you see fit; we've lost all surprise by now!"

"Aye aye, sir!"

"Midshipman Lane!"

"Sir?"

"Detail a prize crew to that lugger, if you please!"

"Aye aye, sir!"

Nettleton had ruined all chance at easily capturing the luggers. If any further attempt was to be made, it would have to be quickly successful. What West would do with Nettleton now, he wasn't sure, but some disciplinary action was certainly in order.

The *Perseverance* had come hard round again, and was just settling on her fresh tack. Ahead lay two of the Spanish merchants; the third had taken refuge in the islands off on the channel's right side. There she would probably heave to until she was sure that the threat was past. Well, thought West, that's not how its going to happen.

"Mr. Tallis!"

"Captain?"

"Come aft here, if you would.

"Aye, sir." A moment's pause.

"The third lugger has, I believe, hidden herself in that forest of shallows off on our starboard side. Her captain undoubtedly knows these waterways far better than I; to bring *Perseverance* in after her would mean the loss of all three of the other craft."

"Yes, sir."

"What I want you to do, Mr. Tallis, is to load the quarterboat and jolly boat with marines and armed seamen. Launch quietly here, and row through those islands until you find her. Where this sloop would run aground, her boats would merely slow. Keep both together, mind you; I doubt you'll encounter much resistance from an old merchant and his family, but it wouldn't do to lose one or both boats in that territory. Assign a prize crew once you've boarded the lugger, then pull back to the ship. Is that quite clear?"

"Quite clear, sir."

"Very good, Mr. Tallis. You may launch immediately."

"Aye aye, sir."

Now West had only the two luggers to be concerned with; Tallis could be trusted with the third.

Ahead, the first of the luggers seemed to be falling back; she must've been hit with one of Nettleton's cannonballs. Crippled and heeling, she would not be difficult to capture. The other, though, was pulling away to *Perseverance*'s port side, and might attempt a dodge into the shallows and then a dash to the shore battery, signaling them to warn of the threat. If that occurred, West might as well sail for the squadron that very night. With warships patrolling the Ria for him, scouts sent to spot him from shore, and a sharp lookout at the fort day and night, he would quickly find himself trapped. No; he had to prevent that lugger from notifying anyone of its comrade's misfortune.

West raised a glass and watched her closely for several minutes; she apparently served as a powder barge, and was en route to a damaged vessel or two—Tripolitan, perhaps, somewhere in the Mediterranean, to provide them with enough gunpowder for defense on her journey to a home port.

"Captain West, Mr. Tallis has launched his boats," called Caswell from somewhere behind West on the quarterdeck. He turned to face him.

There, in the ship's wake, were *Perseverance*'s quarterboat and jolly boat, pulling steadily away from their mother ship's stern, packed full with about seventy marines and fifty seamen. It was an unnecessary show of force; there would probably be no casualties on either side. But West felt that he had better place as much extra manpower as he dared behind each move he made; that insurance might, in some situation, be needed.

The ship was coming upon the nearest of the luggers now, and the time drew nigh when a move would be necessitated.

"Mr. Caswell!" cried the captain, at length. "Put a shot across her bow!"

"Aye aye, sir!"

The gunner was called to the fore maindeck carronade, and he lay the weapon just so that it would fire along her bowsprit. A shot cracked out, accompanied by a double splash near the Spanish vessel as the ball skipped once and then hit the water.

"Put the next one through her side if that ensign doesn't come down in thirty seconds. Just one shot, mind you, and above the waterline; her cargo may well be rice."

That drew a laugh from the men; rice, if saturated in the hold of a ship, would slowly swell so as to split her very seams. The Spaniard either didn't bear that thought in mind or carried a far less absorbant cargo, for she did nothing to haul down her colors. West paused a moment, then said:

"She has made her decision. She's yours, Mr. Caswell."

"Aye, sir. Gunner's mate! Lay a ball across her beam."

"Aye aye, sir."

The second shot brought to the crew's ears the satisfying crunch of splintering wood and shattering timber, and a feeble cheer rose from the maindeck, only to be quieted by Caswell at a prompting look from the captain.

"I'll give her one final chance, Mr. Caswell, and then you may broadside her."

"Of course, sir. Another shot, Gunner's mate."

The next *crack* brought about another shower of splinters, but still the flag did nothing to quit the masthead. West could no longer waste his time with single, petty shots at this lugger; he had another still to catch.

"Mr. Caswell," said he, "You may sink her beneath the waves."

"Aye aye, sir! Port side, run your carriages up!"

There was the comforting rumble of eleven cannons sliding forward on their tackles to be fired. Even West could not help but quicken his stride.

"Hands to the braces!"

"Match set!" cried each of the hands at the guns in turn.

"Fire!"

A thunderous crash deafened even West, who stood now on the quarterdeck, and the very ship beneath his feet lurched slightly in recoil as a gigantic cloud of black smoke billowed up from the port side, obscuring West's view of the lugger. He breathed it in; sulfur. A familiar smell aboard ships in battle.

The acrid black mass lifted like a curtain, to reveal a terrible scene on a splintered stage.

The lugger was now almost entirely dismasted; only her mainmast stood erect, with yards and sails hanging in ruins around it. The vessel was listing heavily to port, rolling her barnacle-encrusted starboard side clear of the water. What survivors there were had started to swim towards the nearby shoals and islands; there was no hope of saving the ship.

Perseverance's crew let out a cheer of victory; West did nothing to quiet them. This time, they'd done something of merit.

"Reload your carronades, men!" cried the captain. "We've another Dago ship to chase!"

At this, the cry became an indefinable roar, though it subsided shortly as the hands moved to execute their orders.

Soon, the guns were set once again to fire.

"Mr. Foster!" West called.

"Sir!"

"Two points a-port!"

"Aye, sir."

"Mr. Caswell!"

"Yes, sir?"

"Stand to your guns; the moment they bear, let loose a broadside."

"Aye aye, sir."

West could see the enemy vessel off the port bow; she had made still more sail, hoping to outrun the clumsy sloop. He changed his mind.

"Belay that, Mr. Caswell. Man the bow chaser."

"Man the bow chaser, gunner!" Caswell echoed

"Aye aye!"

He would see if he could either slow the other craft or force her to surrender by keeping at least one cannon firing at her for the duration of the chase. There, in the forecastle, the gunner's mate would carefully sight each shot, taking into account the rocking of the ship, and reloading as fast as possible. Not only would it demoralize the lugger's crew, but it would empower his own to know that the enemy was under constant and accurate fire. If he had a ship's mortar, that might work as well, but he did not, and so cannonfire would have to suit his purposes.

After another half hour's chase, *Perseverance* finally caught the last Spanish lugger, and forced her, through continued fire, to strike her colors at last. Another midshipman was assigned as prizemaster and a crew sent aboard, and then each vessel was on her way. Now all West had to do was find Tallis.

When the *Perseverance* returned to the spot where the two boats had been launched, there they were again awaiting her. From a distance, West could see that there were prisoners.

A few moments later, the boats' crews were safely aboard, and the prisoners (two Spanish officers) had been quartered below. West allowed his crew to dine; no lunch was taken that day due to the constant chases. Tallis was invited to present his report over a dinner in the captain's cabin.

As Sway brought forth the steaming platters from the galley, Tallis began his tale.

"It was simple enough, really, sir. We could see the enemy's masts as soon as we had pulled away from the ship. So I ordered the crew of the jolly boat to approach from the north in exactly five minutes, and my boat would appear from the east at the same time.

"We came up to the lugger, sir, and they hailed us in Spanish. I don't speak a word of it, sir, so I yelled back, 'Americans, you dogs!', and they tried to set sail. We were faster, though, and we climbed her side—my boat first, then the jolly—and we started to take her crew prisoner. There were the two officers, sir—and I brought them to you. Then there was a woman, an old fat fellow, and about twenty-five able hands. They put up a bit of a fight, they did, sir; but a marine clubbed one with his musket, and they went pretty quietly.

"Did anyone aboard speak English?" West asked.

"Yes. The one officer—the older, I believe—said to us, as we got him into the quarterboat, 'Your fight is with Tripoli, not Spain', and so I said, 'Then why do you persist in attacking our vessels abroad?', and to that he had no answer."

"That was all he said?"

"Yes, sir. That and that he knew we'd never get the shipyards."

West sat up.

"He mentioned the shipyards?"

"He did, sir; said that with the shallows around them and all, that we'd never be able to fire on them, and that at least they were safe."

"Thank you very much, Mr. Tallis," West said, rising. The meal was finished, the story told. "That will be all; if you will send both of the prisoners—under marine guard, of course—to the for'c'stle, I believe I shall now interview them there."

"Aye aye, sir. Thank you, sir."

"Good night, Mr. Tallis."

"Night, sir."

The first lieutenant opened the door, brushed past the marine sentry at attention there, and then proceeded to find the Spanish prisoners as ordered.

West slowly began to pace. These Spaniards might prove to be of some use. They could not only give news of the American war with the Barbary States and that of the English, French and Spanish, but could also provide him with enough information to intelligently and efficiently destroy the shipyards, perhaps as soon as the next day. If what the man had said to Tallis regarding shallows was true, then another method of attacking the shipyards would be needed. What could be done in that case, West could only imagine—but he knew it would be difficult.

He broke his pacing and went to his sea chest, drawing out once again his vast boat cloak. It was time to go on deck; the prisoners would be ready to receive him now.

The sentry outside his door snapped crisply to the vertical as West stepped outside. He had been asleep, most likely. The captain could not have such matters further from his mind.

On deck, night was fast descending on the Ria de Arosa. The air was beginning to cool, and the stars began to emerge from behind their blue veil of daylight.

Tallis loomed up behind him.

"Prisoners ready, sir," he said with a salute.

West did not reply; instead, he knuckled his forehead and began to walk to the forecastle.

As he strode across the maindeck, the hands, surprised at the sight of their captain among them, shrank back into the shadows out of respect. They could sense that he was deep in thought—blood might be running from the scuppers tomorrow, enough of it to cover the deck, but they knew he would act as though every drop were his own.

The fore hatch was off its coamings, and West stepped inside. There, in the shimmering light of a lamp of whale oil, stood four men—two bound, two holding muskets to their shoulders.

West examined the faces of the Spanish officers. One wore a moustache—obviously the younger of the two—and the uniform of a midshipman in the Dago navy. The other sat taller, prouder, stronger, and was denoted as a lieutenant by his clothing. Both men stiffened noticeably at the entrance of this new, dignified American, obviously the captain. These men were not afraid, West knew; only wary.

"Hola. Yo soy el captan del eso bota. Me llamo Lowell West, en la navi de los Estados Unidos de America," West said to them in their native language. At this, they jerked up in surprise, excited to meet an enemy who spoke their tongue. West had introduced himself as the captain of the ship, a commander in the United States Navy. When he had finished speaking, both of the prisoners began to rattle on in rapid Spanish. He held up a quieting hand.

"Forgive me," he said in Spanish. "But I am not fluent in your language."

"I apologize," the lieutenant responded. "I had overlooked that fact. It is very pleasing to me to find someone aboard this ship who understands me."

"I am honored to be considered as such. But, as the situation now stands, we find each other on opposing sides, in a war that must soon be brought to an end. Though I regret committing you such an indignity, it is my duty now to obtain as much information as possible from you." That was the truth; West had nothing at all against the Spanish, and thus found it difficult to treat them as lowly prisoners of war. "Will you cooperate?"

"I will reveal as much as my duty allows. But first; allow me to introduce myself," the lieutenant said. "My name is Armando Zamora, lieutenant in the navy of His Majesty the King of all Spain. This," he said, nodding at his companion, "is Ricardo Hernandez, midshipman in the same service. I have been commissioned to captain a small supply lugger and her sisters, to act as a 'commodore', if you will. My mission was to sail them to the port of Bilbao, to resupply a squadron of frigates due in from the English Channel off Ushant. The British Admiral Nelson, I believe you call him, is making a campaign there now."

So Nelson was slowly beating back the French and Spanish forces that so desperately tried to take their mainland. That was news in itself; but there was more in which he was intersested.

"Have you any news of the American ships in their war with Tripoli?" he asked.

"I have. There were several ship actions yesterday in the Mediterranean, I believe, and American Commodore Edward Preble was beaten only once, by a ship of the line, no less. Your vessels, I hear, are doing extremely well in that theater; a fact which, apparently, due to the present situation, my government did not anticipate."

Ha! That was proof of what Estleman and the War Department had suspected: the Spanish were supporting the Tripolitans in the present war, by attacking the American ships that sailed through their boundary waters. If the lieutenant knew he had given something away, he did nothing to show it; West did not intend on making that plain to him.

"That is excellent to hear, I must say," said West, more politely than he would have were he conversing with his own mother. "You certainly have an efficient naval force as well."

"You are too kind, my good sir."

"I do not exaggerate, lieutenant. Take this very waterway for example. Its shipyards is very well protected indeed." The clinching statement was coming soon.

"It is. The shore battery at Santa Eugenia has excellent vantage for the protection of this waterway—most of the time."

"It does, it does. But I have heard far greater tales of the shipyards itself. Shallows, I believe, surround it almost entirely."

"That is very true indeed; my own luggers found it very difficult to maneuver closely to the shore in that area."

"And there are cannon batteries, artillery pieces, and men, I am told."

"No, that there are not. The shipyards is actually—I," stuttered the man, suddenly realizing how much he'd said.

"Do continue, please," West encouraged casually, trying to mask his intentions.

"No—no, I fear I must not. I have revealed far too much already. To say more would be to violate the bounds of my duty."

"For that I am truly sorry," he responded, once again telling the truth. The lieutenant was a pleasant man; under differing circumstances, West would have spoken with him at greater length. As it was, it was time to take his leave.

"Th-thank you for your most gracious attentions, Captain. I am honored." The lieutenant said haltingly, as the implications of the information West had obtained sunk in.

"And I am honored by your honest, polite, and kindly responses. Good night to you, sir."

"Good night."

With that, West touched his hat, wrapped his boat cloak around him, and emerged into the chill night air.

It was apparently true; the shipyards *was* at the center of such a system of shallows, and West would require an alternate means of attack than the cannon bombardment and simultaneous landing action he had in mind originally. The timing would be impossible if such an assault were to be accomplished at great range; one or the other would probably have to suffice. He would definitely hit the shipyards the following morning, though, regardless of the circumstances. For now, though, he had to sleep.

The next day would dawn all too early.

CHAPTER 8

❀

There was no sunrise the next morning; for hour after hour, the sky remained as black as midnight. A mighty squall had blown up the Ria overnight, clouding the early morning sky and pounding *Perseverance*'s deck with relentless rain and wind. Seas were especially high; the ship shuddered with each new wave. But still she was kept under sail, pushing diligently onward for her objective, a shipyards as yet far out of sight.

West stood alone on the starboard side of the pitching quarterdeck, one arm for himself, the other for the ship, entwined in the hammock netting for balance. His visage was cast upward, at the large, looming mainmast, and her spread of ghostly sails, shuddering and flapping as the wind changed. He was worried about the ship's canvas; if she bore too much, the danger of rigging damage was very real. Time was of the essence, though, if the ship were to reach the promised objective under total cover of the storm. It was quite a frustrating dilemma; in the end, West had the fore topsail set to give his ship better steerage way. Lost canvas could be made up; lost time could not.

Perseverance ran towards the shipyards, clawing her way along through the atrocious seas as the wind sang in the taut weather rigging. West thought it wise to stay underway as long as possible. Ah!

But here was a change. Not much, but a correction for the wind had to be made. He summoned the first lieutenant.

"Wind's coming aft, Mr. Tallis," West said, slowing his speech considerably to make it heard over the wind. When Tallis did not take the cue, he issued the appropriate orders himself. "Aloft there! Send a hand to bear those backstays against the top-brim. Hands to the weather braces! After guard! Haul in the weather main brace! Haul together, now, men! Well with the foreyard! Well with the mainyard! Belay every inch of that."

The wind changed yet again, and the ship began to lurch forward with a fresh rhythm. The alteration was good, they would make better time if the wind held.

"Pass the word for the ship's carpenter!" West suddenly cried, realizing that the crew still did not know where the vessel was headed, or even what to expect there.

The call for the carpenter was taken up round the deck, and soon, the familiar paunchy individual with a grey pigtail and a Scottish accent came rolling aft.

"You sent for me, sir?"

"Yes. All I am going to say to you is this: begin preparations for a battle. A long one. Tell the men and the marines."

"Aye aye, sir."

He faded again into the darkness of the storm. West turned on his heel and retreated to the dryness of his cabin. There was still awhile to go before the shipyards would be in sight.

There, he removed his boat cloak and nor'easter, and lay down on his cot. The exhaustion of the past few days had caught up with him; he tried to fight it off, but it would not remit. Now, he suddenly wanted nothing but to sleep…

As he was on the verge of unconsciousness, he was jarred awake by a sudden, unnatural lurch of the ship. A broadside? No clashing of guns. A collision? No vessels near enough for that. What was going on? Then came a myriad of confused shouts on deck above his head, and the telltale thumping of boots as a midshipman was sent to fetch him.

What on earth could it be now?

A knock came upon the door.

"Come in," the captain said in reply. In the door burst open, and a roughly-saluting, entirely drenched young lad thrust himself into the cabin.

"We're hard aground, sir; hard aground and with two pair of sail on the horizon!"

"Damn and blast it! Now, why wasn't I informed of this sooner?"

"It-it's only just occurred, sir," the boy replied, taken slightly aback.

"I'll come. Hell's bells! Where's my pea jacket?"

In a moment's time, West stood at the usual place on his quarter-deck. His telescope held against his right eye, he gazed out across the grey of the sea to spot the approaching vessels, wherever they found themselves at the moment.

Ah. There they were; two little ketches, clawing their way along through the high seas. They were probably bomb-ketches, judging by their rig. Mortar ships, carrying weapons similar to those used to sink old *Nova*. Was it only a year ago? Less that that? These would have no ammunition aboard, since they were obviously newly launched, and on their way to be loaded. Prizes, then. Little threat there.

West then lowered the glass and directed his attention to the ship's side. Far down below, despite the darkness, he could indeed see that the swirling, frothing water did appear to lighten from its usual deep blue. Shoals for certain; *Perseverance* would have to be refloated somehow. And with the shipyards not far away, smaller vessels would be passing the spot where she was grounded more frequently. That meant more opportunity to be discovered; in times of war, it took little to provoke curiosity. If only one vessel spotted the American ship, went about, and reported her position, it would be over for West. His ship would be sunk for certain.

He had to refloat the *Perseverance*. Only one idea came to mind; he put it into effect immediately.

"Mr. Tallis!"

The first lieutenant detached himself from the darkness somewhere aft of West and responded to this summons.

"Aye, sir?"

"Clear away the boats and find their crews. I want gig, quarterboat, and jolly-boat off the starboard side in a quarter-hour's time. One cable to each. Is that clear, Mr. Tallis?"

"Quite, sir."

"Look lively about it, then!"

"Aye aye, sir."

The orders were given. It was the sloop's port side that was literally stuck in the mud; the boats might be able to free her by hauling her out a-starboard, thus breaking the suction. Sail was changed as well, to aid the boats in their effort. West directed his glass again at the troublesome bomb-ketches. There they were, as yet unawares of the *Perseverance*'s allegiance. Let's hope they remain ignorant of that fact until they are under our guns, West thought.

"Quarterboat away!" came the cry as a detachment of hearty seamen swayed her out to starboard. The gig followed, and then the jolly-boat. A hefty line was cast to each vessel, and then each boat's midshipman ordered the men to pull.

As the seamen strained at their oars, as the cables tightened, West could feel the very fabric of the ship upon which he stood begin to list slightly. Very slightly indeed, but she was moving. He strode to the taffrail.

"Pull together now, men!" he called at the top of his lungs, even over the raging storm. "Pull! Heave at those oars!"

The *Perseverance* jumped very slightly. Progress was being made; she was shifting in the grasp of her earthy foe. If the suction of the mud could not be broken, though, it was all for nothing.

After that, the great vessel did not budge. She was indeed hard aground; stuck fast, held in the unrelenting grip of the shore. The sea bottom simply would not yield; eventually, and West was not sure quite when, the hands had to be rotated due to fatigue. This time he himself took the place of a midshipman in the center boat, shouting encouragement in the men's faces. The blowing, wind-tossed sea did not aid in the effort to remove the ship from her present involuntary anchorage. Conditions were miserable down in the boats; one sailor from the crew of each had to dedicate his time to bailing rather than rowing. But still no further progress was made, and still the ketches edged in closer. What would West do if he was discovered? What *could* he do? Questions poured down like the rain, only to mix, unanswered, with the vast, frothing sea of the unknown. Would he be captured? Would they merely sink his ship, or bother to negotiate for it? His crew? What would become of his crew if the ship was discovered in its mission? The war? The government? The country?

Driven to insane desperation, West wrenched his soaking hat from his head and threw it angrily into the sternsheets of his boat. He stripped off his pea jacket, doing with it the same, and allowing himself to be drenched by the rain and the spray. He looked down at the seaman sitting nearest him, in the boat's bow.

"You there! Get up!"

"Aye, sir!" The man vacated his seat and his oar, standing to take West's place in the bow. The captain sat down on the little section of bench and took the oar in his hands. The other men looked at him wonderingly. What was he doing? Had he gone entirely mad?

West began to pull vigorously at his oar. "Pull!" he shouted. "Pull, and double grog when we're free of this embankment!"

That got them to it. Whether it was the sight of their own captain rowing alongside them or the promise of alcohol in the near future, those oars began to scrape away at the choppy water like never before, straining the cables from the ship nearly to the breaking point. It may have been nothing but his imagination, but West thought he could feel the ship begin to give way once more. At any rate, he could feel her timbers shifting and creaking as force was applied by the boats. Suddenly the ship gave a great lurch, and the boats had to row farther out from the ship to maintain tension in their cables.

West, miserable and wet as he was in the bow of his little boat, did not cease to pull and strain at his oar. The ship simply had to be freed.

There came a sudden, loud popping sound, as though planks were being wrenched from *Perseverance*'s hull, and then the great ship seemed to snap upright again. The suction of the sea floor had been overcome! The ship was now free!

"Recall the boats!" West ordered, standing and resuming his earlier station in her bows. He donned his drenched hat and jacket. "Set all possible sail and bring us round hard-a-starboard!"

In moments, he was back aboard with the boats carefully stowed. His orders were beginning to take their affect; as he stood on the pitching quarterdeck, he could feel the *Perseverance* heaving herself about and settling on her new tack. He raised a glass to look for the ketches. They were off in the same direction, and still making straight for the American ship. It would not be long before their capture now.

"How long until they are under our guns, Mr. Tallis?" called West to his first lieutenant.

"About five minutes, sir, by the casting of the log," he responded.

"Excellent. I'll have her guns loaded and run out along the starboard side; you may fire at will. Strike the false colors when I give the order."

By the time the weapons were loaded, the little boats would be well within range, and then the *Perseverance*'s true allegiance could be revealed and the captures could be affected.

West looked around, and suddenly realized it had stopped raining. The wind was still singing in the taught weather rigging, and the sky black as pitch, but the storm was finally beginning to clear. Once these pesky ketches were disposed of, he supposed, conditions would be right for an assault on the shipyards.

He paced the deck for another long moment, and then he could see that the guns were about ready. Still he paused.

"Run them up!" the gun captains shouted. Now was as good a time as any.

"Mr. Tallis!" called West. "Strike the false colors, run our pennant up the halyard, and open fire immediately!"

"Aye aye, sir!"

At the same moment that the Spanish flag fell from the masthead, the first carronade popped menacingly, and then the whole side went off. By the time the American colors were hoisted, the ketches had gone about and struggled ahead half a cable's length.

Going rapidly into irons, the rear vessel realized her mistake and went about again, only to find *Perseverance*'s starboard side staring her in the teeth. Before she had the chance to make another move, she was torn to pieces by a sudden and violent storm of lead. At that, the other ketch dropped her sails and her colors and waited to be boarded.

CHAPTER 9

❀

"Let's see if we can't spot that objective of ours," said West to the first lieutenant. The entire contents of the package of sealed orders had been revealed to him, and the two men now stood together on the quarterdeck, telescopes probing the now distantly visible shoreline for any sign of life.

"Ah!" announced Tallis, a lump in his throat, "*there!*"

West followed his gesture, and his glass came to rest over a large, low compound constructed mainly of wood and stone. It seemed to jut over the water itself, and off to one side lay the stark white skeletons of several new ships of the line, set on chocks there like so many beached whales. It was the largest shipyards West had ever seen; it must extend a quarter mile down the bank, he thought. As far as he could tell, it was, in fact, unguarded by any permanent means. A little patrol boat could be seen not too far off, but there was nothing to fear from it, as the Spanish colors once again flew, and visibility was low in the aftermath of the squall.

"That's it, all right. Now, the question remains: how close dare we get?" he replied.

"Shall I have the quartermaster bring us a-port, sir?" asked Tallis.

"Yes. And put a stout seaman in the chains who'll keep a steady hand with the soundings," West answered. In a moment, that task was completed, and Tallis looked to the captain for further orders.

West allowed himself to pause, and then gave the one that everyone hade been waiting to hear.

"Mr. Tallis!" he bellowed. "Beat to quarters and clear the deck for action. I'll have her guns loaded on the starboard side, but do not run them out."

"Aye aye, sir!" There was a pause of about five minutes as the customary preparations for battle were made. Then, "Deck cleared for action, sir."

"Very good, Mr. Tallis. Set all possible sail, and port the helm."

In a moment, the *Perseverance* was moving at a good pace across the intervening waters to intercept the patrol boat. If the information gathered from the enemy crewmen and the charts was at all accurate, it would require some delicate calculations. The waterway would shallow very rapidly ahead, and West would have to take care not to run her aground.

This was the real challenge; the navigation of an ever shoaling channel. His hope was simply to be able to take *Perseverance* into gun range and hold her there—but that would be difficult under the given conditions. If that could not be accomplished, then what?

"Leadsman in the chains, sir," said Tallis, reporting back after a moment or two.

"Thank you, Mr. Tallis. Get for'rard to the port chains and be ready to report."

"Aye, sir."

The leadsman had begun to call out his sounding depths.

"No bottom, no bottom with this line!" came the shout. It began well. Somewhere behind the captain, the ship's bell tolled the changing of the watch. There was a pause as the leadsman allowed for the ruckus to cease, then cast again.

"By the deep nine!" the man shouted. Nine fathoms; plenty deep for the sloop's keel, which ran just under two.

"Leadsman!" cried West. "What bottom do you feel?"

Ten seconds before the answer came back.

"Sandy bottom, sir!"

Good. They were still well out beyond the shoaling point, and working their way in. A moment of silence, and then:

"Rocky bottom now, sir, shoaling a little! By the mark seven! Seven fathoms!"

"Quartermaster, three points to starboard." West ordered. It was about time to change sail; if the channel began to drop off quite suddenly, like it was prone to do, West had to be able to handle *Perseverance* at a low speed. He paused for a moment, then plunged into action.

"Take in the tops'ls and topgallants!"

The hands rushed aloft, strumming the ratlines like a mournful guitar as they raced to complete their task.

"Now, Mr. Tallis, wear the ship. Course nor' by west." That would commit him to it, driving the ship in directly at the shipyards. They were still several miles out, so the difficult maneuvering would not come for a little while.

"Nor' by west, sir."

"Send the topgallant masts down! Look sharp, lads!"

The rustle of sails and the clink of ironparts met his ears as the men let down the canvas.

"Set the main and fore topmast stays'ls! Get the fores'l in!"

West walked to the binnacle, addressing the wheelman.

"How does she handle by this sail?"

"Well enough, sir," the quartermaster concluded as he spun the wheel tentatively this way and that, testing the bite of the rudder.

"Good. Delicately, now."

"Aye, sir."

"By the mark five!" called the leadsman again. The shallows were creeping up on them. West strode to the rail and held out his glass. After a moment's pause, he spoke again.

"Quartermaster, two points to port. Steady."

"Aye aye, sir."

The ship was creeping along now, barely moving at all. The low speed was necessary, though, to avoid running aground again in the unpredictable water.

"Three fathoms!"

"One point to starboard."

"Aye, sir."

The tension rose perceptibly.

"By the mark five!"

The channel did not shoal uniformly, then. Rather than being a good sign, this served only to provoke a greater caution from the captain.

"By the deep seven!"

"Quartermaster, half a point to starboard."

"Aye, sir."

Suddenly, there was alarm in the voice of the leadsman.

"Two! Two fathoms!"

"Two points a-port!"

"Aye aye, sir!"

There was scarcely six inches under *Perseverance*'s keel, but she was barely moving across the water. With any luck, the waterway would deepen again in a few moments.

"By the mark three!"

That was something, at least. It would make navigation a bit easier. Still, West detected a certain amount of tension among the crew.

The ship had traveled a good distance in toward the shore, and the shipyards appeared larger in the spyglass now. West studied it with interest; the compound seemed to be extremely busy with the service and outfitting of ships. Directly a-bows was the largest building of the lot, probably the ever-important warehouse in which all of the shipwrighting materials were stored. That would have to be the first target to cannon; next would come the administration facility off to the right, and then the rest of the outlying structures. It could now be seen, though, that officers of the Spanish army patrolled the shores and all of the buildings; that indicated a garrison. West had hoped that, if it was impossible to bring the ship in close enough to use the guns, a landing party could be sent. That would be inadvisable now. If the batteries could not be used to bring down the shipyards, then it was impossible for West to fulfill his orders.

"Two fathoms!"

It was shoaling fast again. Before West had the chance to issue any order, another call came from the leadsman, and one which he dreaded to hear.

"Touching bottom to starboard!" and then, immediately afterwards, "Touching bottom to port!"

"Quartermaster," West ordered, "Give her seven points to starboard and back her off."

"Aye aye, sir."

In a moment, the big ship began to turn in an attempt to wrest her bows from the bottom. Luckily, as the shore was rocky, the hull was not stuck fast, and, after a jerk of the deck, *Perseverance* was on her way again, heading off on a different tack.

"By the mark five!"

There was more freedom here than expected. Delicate care was still required, however, and if West's attention wavered even for a moment, there would be trouble.

"By the deep nine!"

For another half hour, the *Perseverance* heaved herself slowly along, drawing sluggishly closer to her objective. A little while later, though, the channel dropped short, and she touched bottom again, still almost four miles out.

For the rest of that day and most of the night, West attempted several different routes to arrive within firing range of the shoreline, but to no avail. Each moved his ship only a little closer, and then shoaled suddenly. Every time, another, freer passage would be found and followed, until eventually it became clear that the bottom was far too shallow for the *Perseverance* to approach any further or any more directly. It was impossible to draw any nearer, impossible to shell the shipyards from out at sea.

Well after midnight, West, exhausted and visibly discouraged, returned to his cabin to attempt to sleep. He had left Caswell in charge, with instructions to bring the ship out of the shoals and, once in open water, to heave-to for the night as another course of action was considered.

Frankly, he wasn't sure where to turn from here. Any landing patrol, even with the marines, would be easily turned back, and then none would escape the Ria alive, due to the shore battery at Santa Eugenia. If he turned around and fled, unable to complete his mission, he would probably never be posted as a captain again, and his lieutenants would lose their commissions. What alternative was there?

After an hour in his cot, West still could not find solace in sleep. He lit his lamp and sat up, trying to clear his mind. In the end, though, he was resolved to pacing his cabin deck, searching desperately for a way out.

If the ship's cannons could be swayed out into the boats, then perhaps they could be set up against the opposing shore and fired at the enemy. No. The plot would be easily uncovered by the patrol boat before it could be completed, and there was not suitable place for the guns. If the ship could be floated on camels—empty boats lashed to the hull to reduce a ship's draft—then perhaps she could be floated into range. Again, no. Any attempt to fire a broadside under such conditions would undoubtedly dislodge the camels, leaving the *Perseverance* stranded in the shallows.

In desperation, West strode to his desk and unrolled his charts of the waterway, scouring them for a solution to his problem, as though it was they who tormented his sleep. Another hour brought nothing of any worth.

Almost delirious from exhaustion, West finally moved to away his charts and maps and resign himself to defeat. Glancing idly at one map as he rolled it up, he had the vaguely amusing thought that the entire channel was shaped like a half moon, the fort at one end, the shipyards at the other. If only he could connect the two—

And he could. Suddenly it dawned on him, a bright, unifying realization that broke through the crowded haze of his mind like the burning sun—*he could connect the two ends of the waterway!*

Old *Nova*'s demise at the hands of Tripolitan mortar-shellers inspired the soulution to his problem.

The fort!

CHAPTER 10

❀

The next morning, Captain West stood impatiently on his quarter-deck once again, all thoughts of despair aside. He had a plan.

The *Perseverance* tore through the water, thrashing her way along as she crawled rapidly away from the shipyards, making hard for the opposite end of the channel, driving for the sea. Time was finally on the American side—or so West hoped.

"Foremast watch!" he called at the top of his lungs. "What see you direct a-bows!"

"The foaming sea, sir," came the reply. "And naught on the horizon!"

Blast! He might not catch her.

"Deck, there!" came the cry from the masthead, indicating a sighting. "Belay that! I can just make her out, sir, clawing along a good six miles ahead!"

"Very good!" called West, and then, to Tallis, "Set all possible sail, and let's not lose them. Prepare to dip our colors and signal, as discussed."

"Aye aye, sir."

As Tallis rolled aft to give the appropriate orders, West raced forward to have a look for himself. Reaching the futtock shrouds, he legged himself up, and climbed up the full length of the mast.

Reaching the masthead rapidly and hauling his body up, West twined his left arm into the toplines to keep from falling, and then raised a glass.

There was the ketch, just as the sentry had said, driving ahead to the mouth of the Ria. Hopefully, that midshipman would have enough sense to signal when she spotted the *Perseverance*.

And surely enough, as West watched, the little vessel came about, having sighted the American ship. Once signaling distance was achieved, in only a matter of moments, the necessary orders could be given.

"Mr. Tallis!" West ordered, upon reaching the deck.

"Sir?"

"Run this up the signal halyard immediately: 'Heave-to and send commanding officer in boat right away. Await further orders.'"

"Aye aye, sir."

It would be a little while until a reply was possible, but it would all happen soon enough.

After about ten minutes had passed, and the ketch had drawn closer to the ship, Tallis reported back.

"Bomb-ketch acknowledges, sir, and is lowering boat directly."

"Excellent, Mr. Tallis. Reduce sail and heave the ship to. Sway out the nets and prepare to receive cargo."

"Aye aye, sir." The puzzled first lieutenant disappeared once again into the squalor of the 'tween decks to reissue his orders.

In another minute, the boat from the ketch was alongside, and her commanding midshipman climbed aboard. He was a responsible chap, a dark-haired young fellow named Luke Gordon.

"You summoned me, sir?"

"Yes, Mr. Gordon. Mr. Tallis! If the both of you would accompany me to my cabin?"

"Of course, sir."

After initial inquiries about the state of repairs on the captured bomb-ketch and the condition of the prisoners, West drove at his point.

"Now, Mr. Gordon. The *Perseverance* draws far too deep to approach the shipyards from sea. Your captured vessel would probably solve this problem, but for the fact that she carries no mortar shells, and we have not the facilities aboard either vessel to acquire them. Likewise, the ketch is too small to carry any effective number of cannons without considerable damage. Do you follow me thus far?"

"Aye, sir," replied both Gordon and Tallis.

"There is, however," West went on, "a means by which to acquire the necessary facilities. Mr. Gordon."

"Yes, sir?"

"You are to supervise the transfer of the ship's mortars from your vessel to the *Perseverance*. Simply move the mortars themselves; there is no need to remove the mountings, as they will not be needed. Mr. Tallis will see to it that they are received and lashed to the deck—not set up. This sloop is not configured to launch sixteen-inch mortars. Once that is done, Mr. Gordon, I want you to strip down your prize crew to the *barest minimum* and set off for the United States. Is that quite clear?"

"Aye, sir."

"And Mr. Tallis?"

"Aye, sir."

"Report back to me at the completion of your orders. That is all."

The two inferior officers raised their hands in salute, and disappeared into the companion beyond, Gordon flickering an eyebrow at Tallis as they went.

West then donned his coat and hat once more, and went up on deck to oversee the execution of his orders.

On the maindeck, Tallis had the hands at work on the sway rig for the two gigantic mortars; once the smaller vessel was alongside, these would be lowered over and affixed to the weapons, then used as harnesses to bring them to the deck level of the *Perseverance*. Gordon was descending the side to his waiting longboat, and the nearby ketch awaited further orders.

West saw to it that the harnesses were rigged properly (a tiresome task), and then ran a rapid inspection of the equipment that was to be used in the extraction of the mortars from the ketch. Under Caswell's direction, a space was cleared on the forecastle for the storage of the devices, and the starboard watch was engaged in sail drills under Third Lieutenant Nettleton. Foster, the quartermaster, calibrated the rudder cables in his idle moments, and the carpenter gave the hull a careful run-down. The ship was busy in every facet, tingling with anticipation in every ream. Not a soul aboard save the captain knew precisely what was in store, but they all accepted his authority unquestioningly, due to their extreme respect for he and his position.

By the time the sway rigs were completed, the ketch had lain-to alongside, and the crews of both vessels were ready for the operation to commence. Midshipman Gordon supervised the correct attachment of the mortars to their cables, and then Tallis led the crew in hoisting them into the rigging. West admired their skill and strength; these were not light burdens. Once they were held in place high above the deck, he ordered their careful lowering; first the port side, then the starboard. Individually, each mortar casing came to lie, gently, on the forecastle deck, where they were lashed down to prevent damage.

That done, he transferred the Spanish prisoners from Gordon's vessel to his own, where they were placed under guard, and then sent him off with news and mail to the United States. Grog and rum was issued to the ship's company as they watched the stern of the retreating vessel disappear down the length of the channel.

"Mr. Tallis!" West called as the hands ate.

"Sir?"

"Inform the officers: there is to be a meeting in my cabin tonight, four bells precisely. Foster may have charge of the deck; post the usual watches."

"Aye aye, sir."

With that, West retired for a little more planning, and perhaps some sleep.

❦   ❦   ❦

"Officers and gentlemen of the U.S.S *Perseverance*, I now call this council to order," began West, sitting in his cabin with his lieutenants and midshipmen around him. "As you all witnessed yestereve, it is impossible to bring the ship within cannon range of our objective, the Spanish shipyards, which was named as the culminating point of my orders. Due to this unexpected circumstance, an alternate course of action must be determined. I have a proposal to that end, which we will implement as soon as time permits. Consider this your formal briefing; from here out, the men and marines," he added, for the Sergeant was also present, "are to be told only as much as necessity allows. Is that clear?"

West paused before he waded into the thick of it, allowing for nods and grunts all around. The men had just been treated to a meal, so they were ready to do nothing but listen.

"Now, gentlemen," he continued in a lower tone, "we come right to it. As there is no chance of a landing party, due to an army garrison, our only option is to attack from sea, or from afar, each requiring the use of heavy artillery." The tension rose perceptibly, though West was not certain quite why. "As attack from sea has proved difficult or impossible, the only feasible course of action is to mount an assault from some opposing shore with one of two means of artillery at our disposal. There is no shore within cannon shot that would facilitate our removal of the guns from the ship. By what other device, then? By mortar."

"Sir, if you'll pardon the inquiry…" began the first lieutenant. West mimicked a bored look.

"Go ahead, Mr. Tallis," he said.

"We have no mortar shells, as you are certainly aware, and nowhere to erect the mortars we have, by land or sea. I do not view this as an option." He said.

"Mr. Tallis," said West, "in that you are quite correct. We have no mortar shells, nor other ammunition or means to serve our purpose. There is, however, a way to acquire such shells, and an adequate place to mount them.

"The two ends of this waterway, la Ria de Arosa, occur at the source (near the shipyards), and at the ocean (the shore battery). Upon examination of our charts, it is quite plain that the shape of the waterway is that of a 'u', bringing the two points, the fort and the shipyards, relatively close together. Not nearly within cannon shot, mind you; but with enough powder, I am *certain* that a mortar could span the distance."

There was silence as he laid it on the table. Not a soul moved, or even breathed. He spoke again, loudly and harshly in the small cabin.

"I propose, gentlemen, that with a force composed of seamen and marines, we storm the shore battery and fort at Santa Eugenia, thus providing us with the facilities to cast mortar shells and a place to erect the mortars. When the time comes to flee, as surely it will, we will not be hindered by enemy fire from the fort. Well?"

Again, none spoke. Finally, and seemingly with a great effort, the sergeant of marines leaned forward.

"When shall I assemble my men?" said he. The look on his face was one of approval and anticipation; he liked the idea.

Overwhelmingly, the reaction was positive for the plan. In the cabin that night, West and his officers laid down the final plot for the assault, which was to take place at the soonest instant that time allowed. By West's reckoning, that would be only twenty-four hours away.

In that time, the men would see either victory or defeat, reward or demise. It was too short a time for a failure, West decided. He would have to make it a victory.

CHAPTER 11

The officers and men were up with the dawn the following day, planning and preparing for the attack from the very start. As per the captain's orders, none of the hands or enlisted marines were told the particulars of the assault, but, as was typical aboard any ship of war, wild rumors circulated from the beginning.

As for West, he was idle for most of the morning, having carried out his planning the night before. It was now the officers' time to drill the men, and to work out their own strategies. West, though, simply sat in his cabin and familiarized himself with the landscape surrounding the fort, or else drew and polished his blade.

All the while, *Perseverance* ran along through the choppy waters of the Ria, pulling herself rapidly closer to the shore battery. It was imperative that she did not arrive too soon, however; if her presence was noticed before nightfall, the situation could be a bit awkward.

The other facet of command that West had not quite anticipated was the uneasiness experienced when incommunicado for long periods of time. No one aboard the *Perseverance* had had letters or tidings from home for nearly three months now, and that was miniscule compared to the average length of a tour of duty. Even so, on the longest of voyages, one would typically receive periodic mailings and updated orders every month or two. Due to the nature of West's assignment, though, no friendly ships or neutral ports could be contacted for such extravagances. The only thing he could count upon for his return, as far as consistency was concerned, was that Jefferson would still be in office.

At any rate, that was long off, and he had a job to do in the immediate future.

That day was perhaps the longest that West ever knew. All through the daylight hours, sitting idle, directing the movements of his ship and his men, waiting for night to fall. Minutes passed as hours, hours as days. Many times he paced for only a few moments but perceived that he had strode that track of deck for hours. And still time wore on—until night fell, and then things began to happen.

Just as the sun dipped beneath the cliffs and the sea far beyond, West saw it—there, almost beautiful, was the fort at Santa Eugenia, silhouetted romantically against the blazing sky. There was only a quarter mile to sail before the ship reached it; time to anchor.

The fort, though very close in truth, was situated so high above the Ria as to give the impression of being very far away. High above the double-reinforced stone walls flew the Spanish ensign, a symbol of evil to most of the hands, and an invitation of challenge to West and the officers. The fort's structure was pentagonal—two sides faced the Atlantic, one the channel, and the remaining two the shore. Six big forty-two pounders were mounted at interval along each of the seaward faces; of the landward two, only one was guarded. There was a large iron and wood gate on the most inward side of the pentagon, which was protected with two twelve-pounder cannons, set about ten feet up on either side of the gate. Guards patrolled the cannon emplacements on all sides, though they probably seldom expected any trouble. The garrison held therein was probably a very small one, only a regiment or two, due to the fact that the Ria de Arosa was not a popular target for the British, and no American had ever threatened there before.

Aboard the *Perseverance*, the order was given to lay-to on the anchor, and all sail was dropped. She soon lay, scarcely moving, on the outward side of a tall cliff, obstructing her from view of the fort. By this time the sun was well down, and the temperature was beginning to drop. As any sound would carry up the rock face to the battery, orders were now given at a whisper's volume.

"Call all hands, Mr. Tallis," said West, when he though the timing to be appropriate.

"Pass the word among the men: all hands, and attention on deck." Tallis relayed. Instantly, the boatswain and his mates scurried off to spread the order to as many as possible. Swiftly and silently they appeared on deck, filing up from below in line after line. As they arrived, they stood at perfect attention, awaiting the next instruction.

"Marine sergeant!" whispered West.

"Sir!"

"Call your men to attention on the quarter!"

"Aye, sir!"

There was the sound of the marines forming up, nearly three hundred of them.

"Marines at attention, sir, all present and accounted for. Awaiting further orders."

"Thank you, sergeant."

By now, the entire ship's compliment of officers and men stood on the main and quarterdeck, all looking to their captain for instruction. West first began to the enlisted men.

"Gentlemen, tonight we will row together into battle yet again. You have all served me well in the heat of action before, and I have every faith in you that tonight will be no exception. When the order is given, you are to fall out to your boats. Arm yourselves as best you can; but total silence is to be maintained until the last moment. It's cold steel from here, and my officers are instructed to enforce this rigidly. Any man who fires a musket before I do, I'll hang from the main yard. Is that clear?"

A vast murmuring of "Aye aye" was heard from the men.

"Lieutenant Nettleton will have charge of the ship while I am gone, and his crew will remain behind to man her. The officers all have their instructions; I say again, total silence until the first shot is fired. Lower away the boats! Tonight we take the Santa Eugenia Fort!" At that, a cheer was taken up by the crew, but quickly stamped out by all the officers. The men, at least, were in high spirits.

West retreated to his cabin briefly, and buckled his sword belt to his trousers. Out of a mahogany case on his desk he drew two flint-lock pistols and, loading and placing them on half-cock, stuck them in his belt as well.

Emerging from the companion a moment later, he was pleased to see that the quarterboat and gig were already in the water, and the jollyboat and longboat were being lowered out. Tallis and Caswell had taken command of their boat crews and equipped them; the locker was open, the men now bore cutlasses and boarding pikes. For Tallis' men, there were grappling lines with four-fluked hooks on the end (usually used in boarding attacks). Everything was moving along nicely and according to plan.

Meanwhile, on the quarterdeck, the marines were piling into the barge. They would remain at the ship until all the seamen's boats had gone ahead, eliminating the probable patrol boat and clearing the way.

West now noted that the longboat had been cleared away and lowered; that was his charge for the night. He approached the side, gathering his men up and arming them as well. Then, directing them to board, he descended the side as well.

By this time, all of the necessary vessels were assembled, and the attack could proceed as planned.

"All officers, man your tillers! Pull away!" he called at about usual volume, beckoning to move out. "Pull together now, men!"

Slowly, the flotilla cleared the hull of the *Perseverance* and gathered way to move into the main channel. The seamen strained at the oars, but kept their grunts of exertion to themselves. With muffled oars, no sound at all told of their passing.

As the convoy cleared the cliff face, they were suddenly bathed in pale starlight, and the sloshing of the water against their hulls was more distinctly heard. West had scarcely felt so alive; his heartbeat quickened and the hairs on the back of his neck tingled, as always they did when action was imminent. He could smell the very water upon which he rode, cool and crisp, and the strong taste of salt was upon his tongue. Ahead, the waterway narrowed, and the shallows off to the left dropped off. There was a bend not much further on; if there was a patrol boat, that was where it would be.

As he sat at the tiller of the longboat, West could easily see and motion to his other officers, giving him the freedom to pull ahead in the group. He organized the boats into a single file line to meet the possible enemies ahead. If anything, surprise would work to their advantage. The bend was now just ahead, jutting awkwardly out into the river from shore.

As they came round, the first thing that struck West was the fort, glowing with light from the behind the gun emplacements as it perched high upon the huge black rock face straight ahead. The second thing that struck him was the bow section of a Spanish dinghy.

Stifling a cry of surprise, West stove off the vessel with his foot, which undoubtedly surprised the Spaniard guards inside very much. The oarsman turned around in the little boat, and yelled at the sight of the American invaders.

That was all that West allowed him. In a flash of bright reflected moonlight, he silenced the unfortunate man with a cutlass blade to the throat. None of the sailors were allowed to speak either, for, just as West raised his arm for another strike, three crewmen from his own boat poured into the other and made short work of the remaining witnesses. West wiped his blade and sheathed it, then leant back and took the tiller once again. His oarsmen resumed their stroke, and the little party continued ahead.

At the base of the cliff upon which the battery was perched, the shore flattened out into a little shelf at which a crude dock was constructed, presumably for the Spanish boat and other supply vessels. Here, West ordered "up oars" and piloted the longboat in, mooring it at the end of the dock. The other officers followed his example, and soon all had disembarked and stood on the shelf, arraying themselves into what formations they would for attack, and then seating themselves on the hard ground to wait for the marines. Caswell went back in a half-empty boat to give the go-ahead.

In only moments, the deep blue of the channel across the way was interrupted by the wake of *Perseverance*'s barge, delivering a quarter of the ship's marine compliment to the specified shore. Depositing them there, it went round for more, embarking them upon the same spot. Soon, the last load was on its way, and behind it came Caswell in his vessel, bearing a very special cargo.

As the second lieutenant's boat drew up to the pier, it could be seen that it rode very low in the water; as two of the landside seamen moored it, the great black shape of a nine-pounder cannon was discernable, along with its partially dismantled carriage and about two hundred shots' worth of powder and grape shot. A massive groan rose from the crew at this unwelcome sight; it was they that would pull, push, or drag the gun up the winding trail for use at the gates of the fort.

"Mr. Caswell," ordered West when the boat was secure. "See to it that your cargo is unloaded and made ready for transportation to the fort."

"Aye aye, sir."

"Sergeant," he said, now turning to the nearby gaggle of marines. "Form up your men and order them to fix bayonets. We will move very shortly. Mr. Tallis, where are you?"

"Here, sir!" came the reply, and the senior lieutenant materialized out of the darkness.

"Call the men to attention, and look smart about it. Arrange for a detachment of them to deal with the gun, and spread the grape shot and powder around as evenly as possible. I'll have a rearguard and a vanguard of marines, and the men may march along between. The cannon is to be in the center of the pack, so to speak. Is that all quite clear?"

"Quite, sir."

"Carry on, then."

"Aye aye, sir. You men! On your feet! Johnson, Foster, come deal with this powder. Hodges, pass round the shot. Fall in, then! Look alive!" In a moment, the party was ready to move. West took his place between the vanguard and the column.

"Vanguard, forward march!" he called. When they had drawn ahead a few paces, he followed up with, "Sailors and officers! Forward march!" and finally, "Rear guard! Forward march!"

As they set off along the steep trail that wound its way up the rock face, zagging this way and that among the craggy boulders, West checked the sky. There was no moon, which would only act to his advantage, and the stars were out in force tonight. He found himself amazed at the sheer volume of them; in Boston, with all the oil lamps and chaise lights, one could hardly see a single one. But here they blazed gloriously, freely, dancing upon the trail ahead, disappearing into the brush alongside. By the feel of the air and the weight of his watch, he assumed it must be well after eleven 'o clock, and it was likely to be over an hour's march up the cliffside.

The ground beneath his feet was pockmarked and worn, but not rocky. At the moment, the incline was fairly low; the going was easy, but the climb and the terrain would both intensify before the ascent was through. In some places, West could see recent signs of Spanish activity; broken whiskey bottles, spilled gunpowder, and all the usual trinkets left behind by careless (or carefree) soldiers. Evidently, there was a patrol down this path, by day or night, but the vanguard would deal with any trouble that could be encountered.

As he climbed and the moments wore on, his feet numbed, as naturally they would, but his senses sharpened. West could fell the familiar old thrill of excitement at the thought of seeing true action again, of risking reputation—and life—to do his duty, to gain glory, and (what was really the point), to justify himself in his own eyes.

They plodded monotonously onward for another hour and a half, sweating and panting by the end, and then arrived at the top of the cliff, with the road stretching out before them to the fort. Off to each side there were thick forests that began a few feet off the trail, leaving a shoulder to the gravel portion of the road. At the road they finally stopped, having come a long way already, and redistributed their burdens. After a quarter hour's rest, the captain knew that it was time to begin the attack.

"Pass the word for Mr. Tallis, Mr. Caswell, and the sergeant of marines," said West, standing off to one side of the road. The air was fresh and thin, and smelling vaguely of recent rain. West though that he might enjoy returning to Spain someday on friendlier terms.

"Aye, sir?" That was Tallis and the rest of them, approaching him expectantly. West looked from his officers to the scattered seamen, and then back to the officers. He was pleased to note that, despite the exhaustion felt by all proceeding the march, officer and man alike had an energetic gleam in his eye, and a slight but present wish to draw blood. West felt suddenly alive again, his senses alert; action was now very near.

"Thank you, gentlemen," he said to them. "A quarter of a mile down this road lies the fort. You each have your orders? Good. Mr. Tallis, you may take your detachment of seamen off of the road immediately."

"Very good, sir. Good luck, sir," replied Tallis eagerly, and set about rallying his men. About a third of the sailors leapt to their feet eagerly, brandishing their pikes and cutlasses and forming into the ordered lines. In a moment, they had disappeared off the road and into the trees, running parallel to the road in the direction of the fort.

"Sergeant, divide your men as discussed, and depart at my order."

"Aye aye, sir," he responded with the same enthusiasm, hurrying off to split his men in half.

"And you and I, Mr. Caswell, shall take the remainder of the men, as discussed."

"Aye aye, sir. Shall I arrange for the cannon, sir?"

"Very good, Mr. Caswell."

"Aye aye, sir."

The marines, one half of their volume commanded by a lieutenant, the other by the sergeant, now stood in the center of the road, ready to move at a moment's notice. It was well after midnight by now, West observed. That moment drew nearer every passing second.

"All hands! All hands!" called Caswell to the remainder of the ship's company. "Stand to attention, now! Shoulder your pikes and lay-to on that cannon! Look sharp, I say!" Once all the men were assembled and silent, he turned to the captain. "Ready to move, sir!"

"Thank you, Mr. Caswell," West acknowledged, then paused, looking at each man. They seemed ready enough; nothing he could say would further prepare them for the action ahead. They were true navy seamen now, and had seen enough of battle in the past to know their places. It was time to go.

"Move out!" he ordered, and the column began to march along the road, he at its head. After only a little while, they sighted the fort dead ahead, and the sailors and half of the marines broke off of the trail and headed into the brush to the left of the main way. The remaining marines continued on the same tack, slowing their pace considerably, as to fall behind the rest of the men.

The forest was alive with noise at this time of the night, sounding of crickets and frogs and some species of creature that West had never heard before. Underfoot, the ground was slogged with mud and tangled clumsily with vines and undergrowth. The trees were densely packed. By no means was the going easy, as the men had to break rank to move effectively, but still it was rapid. The gun was the largest concern now; several times it caught itself on one of its trunnions and had to be hacked loose from the mass of plant life in which it was entrapped. Its bearers had to be rotated often, which proved further delay, and it was consistently last in row, though West attempted to keep it in the center of the file to prevent its loss. Eventually, however, the company reached the end of the woods, about a hundred feet from the fort's outer wall, and all fell instantly silent.

The battlements appeared hugely aloof and impenetrable from their position in the forest, and the gate, which lay ahead and to the right, seemed to occupy at least twice the length of the road, and thrice its height. On either side of it were the yawning mouths of the cannons, silent for now, which would soon erupt upon them. On the top of the high battlements, sentries could be seen patrolling, and occasionally a laugh or a snippet of Spanish could be heard. Care would be necessary to ensure that the plan was not foiled through negligence.

Swiftly and silently, under Caswell's direction, the cannon was placed on its carriage, and a space was cleared for its recoil. The tackles were run around two sturdy trees to prevent them from tearing loose, and the powder and shot piled nearby. The muzzle was laid directly at the closed gate.

Slowly, as the men and marines under West's command waited in silence, the night matured, and the darkness began to thin. The sergeant's orders went into effect at sunrise, and then the fighting would begin.

Slowly, reluctantly, as though it knew the carnage that it would probably bring, the red Spanish sun looked through the trees, beginning to melt the icy black of the sky above. The stars began to fade, and West began to listen.

At first, only the faint chirps of the crickets and the low footfalls of the pacing Spanish sentry could be heard, but then, softly at first, but strengthening in intensity and volume, another sound revealed itself. The footfalls of many, accompanied by fife and drum playing "Yankee Doodle". It was the marines, and they were executing West's orders perfectly.

"All right, Mr. Caswell," whispered West, addressing the indefinite shape to his left. "You may put your man in place." The second lieutenant turned and muttered something to a stocky sailor nearby, and the man began to creep to the edge of the woods. He waited until the fort's sentries patrolled the opposite end of the wall, and then dashed silently out to the fort's outer face. Slowly and quietly the man crept around to the gate of the fort, grasping with tender care a canvas sack. When he reached the first of the gunports on the near side of the gate, he sank down onto his knees to wait, his head resting against the stone of the battlment. Several times he looked at the muzzles of the cannons protruding ten feet above his head, and then gauged the weight of his sack using his hands.

The marines could just be made out now, marching solidly along the road to the fort, unafraid, playing their music as bravely as could be. Suddenly, as the sun rose still further, a shout from the wall indicated that they had been seen.

In a flash, there was the sound of a muster bell, calling the garrison to arms. The two cannons overlooking the road were drawn back and loaded. As soon as they poked their heads back out of the ports again, the American waiting directly under them opened his parcel and removed several hefty stones. Aiming carefully, he threw one of them up at the first cannon. It simply glanced off the muzzle with a light *twang* and fell to the ground below. He made the attempt a second time; this time the rock hit its mark, diving into the yawning mouth of the cannon and hesitating there at its lip, just barely visible in the early morning light. That accomplished, the man proceeded to do the same to the other gun, though it required a few further attempts. He then darted into the woods, unseen, on the other side of the road, where more dark shapes could now be deciphered.

As the marines drew within gunshot, several snipers appeared on the rim of the outer wall, firing wildly at this new foe. It was clear that they would save the first cannon shot for a closer one, in order to prevent any chance of a miss. Still, onward marched the marines.

About two hundred feet from the gate, the marines halted, but the music continued to play. In the gunports, the muzzles were shifted to acquire a better aim. They were about to fire…

With a sudden, resounding *bang*, both of the cannons rent their barrels violently, causing the breeches to break and most of the gunners to be killed, West thought. In the barrels, the balls' progress had been momentarily impeded by the tiny stones hurled there by the American, causing them to backfire and the carronades themselves to explode. Thick black smoke marred the sunrise; the Battle of Santa Eugenia had begun. There was now no danger whatever to the marines, who dropped first rank to fire. They did not unleash a volley, though the Spaniards continued to fire their small arms.

Suddenly, and with a great yell, a third of *Perseverance*'s crew, with Tallis at their head, exploded out of the forest to the right of the road, hurling their many grappling lines up onto the battlement at they did so. Before the enemy had time to respond, they began to climb, most scaling the wall with ease, though a few were shot or pitched off by the Spaniards. As they reached the top, a clash of steel could be heard, along with some shouts and a few assorted gunshots. It was clear by the pandemonium inside that the American invaders were pushing towards their objective: the gate.

As yet, each of the principle players in West's elaborately choreographed battle plan was doing his job admirably; but now would come the real test.

With a sudden, unexpected *thunk*, the fort's mighty gate was thrown open by the American sailors, amid shouts and curses from the Spanish with whom they fought. Scarcely had the way been cleared then the Americans threw themselves at the ground with their hands over their heads. Bewildered but determined, their Dago combatants rushed to shut and bar the gate.

"Fire!" West shouted all of a sudden, and the great cannon that lay in the trees to the left of the fort gave a great bellow, mowing down half a dozen Spaniards with its devilish grape shot. The marines let loose a volley at precisely the same instant, and then, once the air was momentarily clear of lead, West ran out from his hiding place in the forest, drew his cutlass, and screamed.

"Charge!" he yelled, and instantly the call was taken up by the seamen that waited behind him and the marines on the road, who began to pour through the open gate and into the fort.

West's adrenaline surged within him as he ran forward, mustering all his strength and bravery to lead the men through the broken defenses. A surprised Spanish face greeted him as he bolted into the stronghold, and he slashed at it with all his strength, it went down with a cry. Around him, the air was pierced with screams, and punctuated with gunshots and the constant clash and scrape of steel. He found himself rushing forward yet again as more and more seamen pushed into the fort, followed by the marines, shooting and bayoneting all in sight. He lost himself in the chaos of battle.

A Spanish army officer, recognizing West as an important enemy leader, raised a pistol to fire, but the American was faster. Whipping a flintlock from his belt and raising the hammer from half-cock, he took a step forward and shot the man in the forehead. He stuffed that gun back into his belt and, seizing the other, let go another ball into a mass of enlisted men, whom the marines pounced on duly. Again he found himself at grips with a Spanish swordsman, and again he struck the man down.

Ahead of him lay the commons of the fort; a squat main building containing administrative offices, food stores, powder, balls, and a guard house. Beneath the ground upon which he stood there was probably a foundry and a furnace, with which to manufacture ammunition from lead and heat red-hot shot. The flagpole in the center of the citadel still bore the Dago flag.

Suddenly, his left shoulder stung with a burning pain. He spun around just in time to see a soldier about thirty feet behind him lower and begin to reload a musket. Instantly, West was on the man with his cutlass. The fellow was quick, though, parrying with the barrel and swinging the stock of the gun. Just as he raised his arms to hit West in the stomach with it, he fell at a ball from behind. Another man sprung up in his place, though, and another and another, so that West soon ached with every move he made.

He engaged what seemed to be dozens of people. Some, he would kill, others would fall victim to stray bullets or valiant seamen. For hours (it seemed) they battled, the din of war surrounding and consuming him, burning in his eyes and driving his hands forward; parry, jab, now lunge. He slew another of his enemies. As he looked for the next, he felt a gentle hand on his shoulder. He spun around, jaw set, eyes blazing, blade extended.

If Tallis had not withdrawn his hand, it might've been cut off. As it was, though, seeing the first lieutenant of his ship shook the captain out of his battle rage, and forced him to look around. Black smoke rose from several buildings and cannons surrounding him, and the ground was littered with bodies of the dead and wounded as far as he could see into the fort. Overhead, the Spanish ensign still flew proudly; of course, thought West as it struck him for the first time. He would only attract further Spanish troops if he removed the flag. He must be careful not to get too hasty.

Off to one side stood a small but fearsome party of American sailors and marines, organizing what prisoners there were into several groups based on degree of injury. The vast majority of the American force was sitting or standing near the well, drinking their fill of water but scarcely speaking. It had been a victory hard won.

Tallis, standing there before West with Caswell at his side, looked awful. His uniform appeared as though it had been put on in the dark aboard a rocking ship and not readjusted since. His gold lace and buttons were torn and missing in some places, his hat was crushed, and the sheath for his cutlass bent at an uncomfortable angle. He finally raised his hand to his hat in salute and breathed:

"Santa Eugenia fort taken, sir."

"Ah, excellent, Mr. Tallis. See to it that the men are drinking plenty of water, and that the wounded are tended," he responded. He could just do for some water himself.

"The prisoners are taken care of, sir; Mr. Caswell has seen to that. Ah—are—if you'll pardon my asking, sir, are you all right, sir?"

West looked down at himself. He did indeed look horrific. His uniform was as torn as the lieutenant's, if not more so. What's more, his hat was missing, and he was splattered with blood over a good deal of his clothing, both his own and his foes'. He suddenly remembered his shoulder, and the pain returned anew. He examined it briefly. Not a bad wound at all; it was simply grazed lightly, scarcely beneath the shirt, and bleeding a little. The worst part was the sting.

"I am in excellent health," lied West. Aside from his gunshot wound, he ached horribly and his throat burned for water. "Carry on, thank you." He saluted and moved off toward the well. There, he drank about a full bucket of cool, clear water, and poured some over his injured shoulder. Refreshed, he moved off through the fort to attend to his duties.

"Cap'n, sir, here's the man to surrender to you," called a foremast hand from somewhere over near the prisoners. The poor officer he held was obviously not the ranking one in the fort, but probably the topmost Spaniard alive at the moment. He spoke thick, gritty English in a raspy moan.

"Keepton West?" he asked. West nodded. "I must here surrender the Santa Eugenia fort to you. Pleeze my sword accept as token of our official surrender." Here, he extended the hilt of his cutlass and bowed his head. Respectfully, West took it with a nod, and dismissed the man.

He next made a move to investigate the administration buildings in the center of the keep. The main office (West did not pretend to know the Spanish title associated with it) was very large; this he took up as his own, as well as the residence directly above it. It was nearly the end of March; tonight would be the first time in nearly six months that he would sleep ashore.

Once his affairs were in order and he had sent for a few of his belongings from the ship, he saw to the arrangement and proper treatment of the prisoners, as well as the distribution of the food stores. Realizing that he had not eaten in nearly two days, he called for his personal attendant.

"Mr. Sway!"

"Yes, sir?"

"Would you be so kind as to prepare me a meal? The best, if you would please."

"Of course, si—Aye aye, sir."

"I'll eat in half an hour's time, Sway."

"Yes, sir."

And with that, he was off like a shot to find the officers' stores in the fort's cellars.

As for West, he was incurably exhausted. He had scarcely slept for several days, and the battle had not aided his condition. Just then the surgeon came up from the foundry, where the wounded had been laid. With a weary wave of the hand, he motioned the man over.

"Captain, sir," said Louis, the ship surgeon, upon noticing West's wounded shoulder. "Are you hurt?"

"Not badly," replied the captain. Louis bent down to examine the area, tearing away the broadcloth of West's uniform as he did so. West almost stopped him, but then realized that this jacket (and the stockings, breeches, and shirt that went with it) could never be worn again anyway. His second uniform would have to suffice from now on.

"No, 'tisn't bad at all," said Louis as he straightened again. "A bit of a creasing, a nasty little burn from the shot itself, and substantial bleeding. Missed the top of the clavicle, though it may have chipped her a bit. A bit of bandage should do the trick."

With that, the man reached into a pocket in his bloodstained apron and removed a roll of white gauze, wrapping it quickly around West's shoulder, tightening it, and then affixing it there with a safety pin. As he finished tying off the loose ends, West requested a formal report.

"Well, sir," Louis began, standing to attention with the bandage finally done. "There are about ninety wounded Spaniard officers and men, and more than a hundred and twenty dead on the enemy side. We've suffered substantial casualties as well: seventy wounded marines, forty dead, and thirty-nine wounded sailors, eighteen dead. That makes for about a hundred and nine wounded, fifty-eight dead on our side of things. Dismal when you look at it right off, sir, but downright splendid when put in perspective."

Indeed it was. West was sorry to hear that so much American blood had been shed, but it was far less than might've been expected in consideration of the odds. The company of a single sloop of war had overwhelmed the entire garrison of a Spanish fort, and less that a hundred and fifty men had been wounded. It was a tribute to the American sailors and a credit to the marines, he decided, though he felt the loss deeply. It might've been much worse, he reminded himself.

"Thank you, Mr. Louis. You may tend to your wounded," said West finally, dismissing the surgeon.

"Quite, sir," he replied, and disappeared into the foundry once more. Behind him, West heard a soft voice offer him the first reward that was to be reaped through all of his adventures in Spanish waters: "Dinner, sir."

"Thank you, Mr. Sway. I will come straight away."

"This way, sir."

The captain's attendant led him to the officers' dining room in the garrison buildings; a fine little space with a low ceiling and well-adorned walls. The furniture was nicely handmade; if the delicacy was half as good, West would have an excellent night of it.

The food was, indeed, exquisite. Fresh roasted chicken in garlic sauce and herbs, a stuffed potato served over Spanish rice, and an odd but delectable little pastry for dessert. The wine, a deep burgundy, was full and rich, and West drank deeply (but not heavily) until he was satisfied. He ate like a rabid hound, devouring every morsel on his platter with astounding rapidity, and then mumbling for more as he finished the final mouthful. Sway brought in a second portion of the chicken and a steaming bowl of rice, and West felt instantly ravished once again. He ate the new helping as rapidly as the first, and then sat back with a smile and a sigh, feeling very full indeed. Motioning that Sway could finish the leftovers (of which there were plenty), he stood and went out of the dining room.

By this time, the sun was falling from the sky, and the hands had finished their evening meal. West hurriedly arranged for them to be quartered in the barracks that were not in use for the prisoners, and posted a large watch to keep an eye on the road at night. The ship's nine-pounder had been run up behind the gate to afford some protection until the original cannons had been repaired. Leaving Caswell as officer of the watch, to be relieved by Tallis at the next change, West sought his own quarters for some much-needed rest.

West stripped off his tattered uniform and laid it aside, confident that it could never be worn again. Donning his usual sleepwear, he crawled beneath the linen sheets of this strange Spanish bed, stranger still to him because of the fact that it was ashore. Tomorrow, the real work would begin, he thought, and the mortar shells would be cast. As for the die, it was already cast and read: he would destroy the shipyards and escape, or be killed by Spanish troops. It was very simple.

As he drifted off to sleep, he found that he missed the groaning of the ship under him, and the harping of the wind through the rigging. It seemed oddly still, and he missed the motion of the sea under the keel.

He missed, too, the security of his twenty-two broadside guns.

CHAPTER 12

The sun galloped across the rims of the Spanish cliffs, running along the flat plains and up the walls, splashing across the bed of the man in the large room above the garrison. He did not like the sun today, and so he rose and drew the curtains.

West was in a black mood that morning, and none, not even he, could tell you why. He snapped at Sway when his breakfast was brought, and at the midshipman that reported on the night's uneventful watch. Again poor Sway felt his wrath as he was dressing himself, and then it was Tallis' turn, making his report on the prisoners.

Eventually, with a dark scowl marring his face, the captain emerged from his quarters in full uniform, this one free of battle scars. He looked out over the commons of the fort, frowning heavily at nothing in particular. He walked to the gates and scowled down the road a ways, then turned and scowled still harder at his fort. Finally, when he had just about scowled himself out, he contented himself with a dissatisfied sneer, which some thought to be worse.

"Mr. Tallis!" he called, his face still harsh. "Have the mortars arrived from the ship?"

"They've just been landed, sir, and we'll have them here in an hour."

"Good," he said, but did not look as though he meant it. "Have the hands broken their fast?"

"No, sir, they have not."

"Well, hop to it, man! I want the ship's company fed and ready to work by the time those weapons arrive. Better see precisely what there is to eat round here."

"Aye aye, sir."

In another hour, as promised, the mortars were at the gates, which were swiftly opened to admit them. Along with the mortars came further powder and cannonball supplies, as well as a good deal of the boatswain's stores and some wood for the carpenter. The latter would be used for necessary repairs to the structure of the fort, and setting up a pair of mountings for the mortars. As soon as the men were fed, West started them at work.

He had the mortars and all the supplies necessary for their handling placed over near the wall facing the shipyards, where they would later be used. Then, the carpenter set to work on the mountings, and the hands were instructed in the basic use of the foundry for casting balls and shells. The facilities were primitive, especially concerning such complicated things as mortar shells, but adequate. Experimentally, a small number of balls were heated to be red-hot and fired from the waterside cannons, in case of a patrol vessel.

As West was overseeing the forging of the first shells for the mortars, a cry was heard from somewhere behind him. He turned and ran into the commons area. There was an enlisted man lying on the ground there with his throat cut, and another standing over him and pointing at the fort's gate.

"There, sir, there!" he shouted. West looked, and saw a Spanish officer climbing the wall along the side of the gate, a makeshift dagger held in his teeth. A few shots were heard as the American marines attempted to kill the escaping prisoner, but the balls ricocheted off the stone wall to either side of the fellow. If he was allowed to get over the wall, he would be free to break for the woods, and then they would never see him again. Spanish reinforcements would be called for, and the fort retaken. West could not allow that to happen.

Stepping to the other side of the poor sailor's body, West drew both of the pistols from his belt. Cocking the one in his right hand, he fired—the shot went awry. He dropped it and switched the other gun to that hand, raising and cocking it as he did so. He took careful aim—the man had nearly reached the top—and squeezed the trigger. The fellow started to fall before the echo of the gunshot died away, but recovered himself and continued up the wall very quickly. He had not been hit, but had lost his grip on the stone.

Cursing his aim under his breath, West wrenched a musket from the hands of a nearby marine, but by the time he raised the weapon, the Spaniard had reached the top of the wall and gone over. That was that; the fellow would rally another nearby garrison to retake the fort in only a matter of days.

"Blast it!" West cried, flinging the loaded gun back at the startled marine, who caught it too near the trigger guard. The weapon discharged harmlessly into the air, punctuating the captain's remark. He would have to rush the production of the ammunition, as the retaliatory Spanish force would be upon them very soon, perhaps even the following afternoon. The shipyards would have to be destroyed very rapidly.

Soon, a few shells had been manufactured, and were ready to be tested. The carpenter had finished with the mountings for the mortars, and the great yawning barrels were now set within them. West stood to the side, supervising the loading process.

The first shell was lifted to the top of the mortar barrel, where it was held momentarily as both fuses were lit. Once he was certain that neither flame would go out, the sailor slid the spluttering ball into the mortar, dropping flat to the ground as he did so to avoid being hit. After a moment's pause, a great scream was heard, and the ball rocketed out of the barrel and over the battlement, exploding only feet above the wall and showering the nearest marines with hot gunpowder rather than shrapnel.

West's mood was not improved. The inner fuse would require less fuel, while the quick match on the outside needed decidedly more. Timing was another concern; with the slow match nearly passing the quick fuse, proper distance would never be obtained before the shell exploded.

"Alright, master's mate," West said to the seaman in charge nearby. "Let's try an eighth inch less on the quick, and a thimble less powder. A fourth more on the slow."

"Aye aye, sir," the master's mate replied, kneeling over the second charge to load it with the proper combination of fuel and fuse. Once it was done and sealed, he laid match to it again and, taking care that both lines remained lit, he dropped it into the leftmost mortar.

This time, the shell got nearly two miles away (by the captain's guess) before it detonated, and there a nice spray of shrapnel could be seen.

"Another eighth inch more on the quick, then, and a penny's worth of powder."

"Aye aye, sir."

The third charge was another improvement upon the second, and the fourth better than even that. With each successive attempt, the distance attained by the shell before explosion was greater, and the spread of the lead shrapnel and flaming powder at combustion increased. Progress was slow, but being made nonetheless. Now that the master's mate had all in hand, West put Caswell in authority there and moved on to oversee the reinstitution of guns over the fort's road side, lest attack come unexpectedly from land. The men, under Tallis' instruction, has arranged a block and tackle over the gate, and had lifted the gun chocks off the trunnions and into the air. They were in the process of positioning them when West heard a shout from behind. He turned instantly to meet the assailing cry.

A terrified seaman ran up to him, panting for breath shaking in fear. West was alert at once; it was not over nothing that veteran seamen became upset.

"What's happened, Mr. Hunter?" he asked. The man took a moment to recover himself.

"It's — sir — I — don't — know — you — better — come see — for — yourself." He panted wearily. West followed as he turned to lead the way, a sense of urgency and despair growing in his heart.

The man led the way into the food cellar, where he and West acquired torches, and then onward into the sick ward, which lay more than twenty feet underground. There, many men, Americans and Spaniards alike, were treated for their ills by the ship's surgeon. Upon recognizing the captain, the surgeon approached, his brows furrowed and his eyes wide.

"Yes, Mr. Louis?" asked West anxiously.

"I was treating four men, all sick of the same illness since before we arrived, apparently. I was never sure what ailed them—symptoms I'd never seen. The other men were afraid of being laid near them, kept mumbling something in Spanish." He explained, leading West deeper into the bowels of the ward. Eerie patches of light splashed here and there from the ventilation holes cut through the rock above. "and I thought nothing of it—a fever, curable through rest and good whiskey. Rum perhaps. But today, sir, I realized it was more than that."

They had reached the end of the chamber, where four figures lay side by side. Two were obviously dead, the others not far from joining them. West began to walk closer to them, but the stench drove him off. It was not the stench of death, it was something else—a smell that West had not detected before.

"And then today two of them died." Louis continued, in a hushed tone. He had begun to sweat like mad again. "And I came over to examine them. Well, sir, I took one look and I realized what the other Dagos had been saying."

West realized it too, just then, and extended his torch arm to get a better look. Louis continued.

"They were saying, *el Muerto Negro*, sir,"

West's vision narrowed and his pulse hastened. In the pit of his stomach he felt a knot of despair, a knowledge of certain death that would not go away. He tried to concentrate of the surgeon's words, and yet he barely heard them.

"They were saying, *the Black Death*, sir!"

West's blood ran cold. Marring the light brown of the skin of the dead men were terrible, misshapen black splotches, swollen and hor-rifying to behold. The Black Death. Plague.

West struggled to free his handkerchief from his pocket as one of the surviving plague patients extended his arm towards him, clawing at the air. Frantic, West kicked the arm down and turned, his head spinning, his handkerchief lifted to cover his nose and mouth. In silence and desperation, he led Louis up out of the pitch-black hell of the medical ward and out into the sunlight. There he dropped the lit-tle bit of cloth and spoke.

"No one is to come in contact with you, your assistants, or your patients until the problem is eradicated. Is that clear?"

"Aye, sir." Louis gulped.

"I want all of these men brought up into the fresh air. You are to take them outside the confines of the fort and set up there, down-wind of this place, in hopes of putting an end to the spread of this thing. Food and supplies will be brought out to you, and tarps erected if it should rain. Under no circumstances is any man to enter the fort unless he is well!"

"Aye, aye, sir," he answered, decidedly pale in the midday light.

"Get a move on, then!" ordered West, shivering as he returned the man's salute. When all of the medical supplies and the patients were ready to be moved, West ordered all unaffected hands to fall-in near the watering well to keep them out of Louis' way. First, all of the sur-gical tables and supplies were carried out, and then the patients followed one by one, some under their own power, some assisted by others. When the entire ghastly entourage had filed by, the captain set the men to work again.

Nothing but problems had arisen since the capture of the fort for West and his men, and by the time plague had been discovered, many were keen on departing with all speed.

West decided at that point to return to his cabin for some much-needed rest. Abandoning his crew to their duties, he slipped off to his chambers to collect his thoughts.

There, sitting at his desk with his neckcloth loosened, his belt let out, and his hat removed, West leaned his head upon a weary arm and shut his eyes. For a few moments, he sat in a state of relative bliss, escaping all his responsibilities and plots, fleeing the fort for America in his mind's eye. Then the doubts returned, coupled with an acute awareness of all the numerous aches and pains he suffered throughout his tired body. More than all else, his feet throbbed and his leg muscles felt thin and stretched. His head hurt terribly; but his mind was so fogged with other things he scarcely knew it.

Eventually, he brought himself back to reality. There was still much to be done with regards to his orders. Ah, tiresome, irksome orders! He had grown quite sick of them by now; what relief he'd feel simply to abandon his filthy orders and return home alive, away from this hell. But he could not. If he returned unsuccessful, he'd have dealt his naval career a mortal blow. That he could not afford; what other occupation would there be for such a person? Court-martial would follow, and disgrace, if not death for treason. No, again the conclusion was that he must not fail. The presence of plague within the fort was an unwelcome shock, but it would have to be dealt with as time permitted. And what of retaliation? If the Spaniards attempted to retake the fort—which they inevitably would, West decided—then it would be a fight to the last man.

His thoughts were interrupted by a tap on the door.

"Yes?" he asked. A foredeck hand bowed entrance.

"Messenger, sir, with a letter for you. We nearly shot him, we did, sir, 'cept he raised a white flag. Figgered we ought to hear him out, anyway. He's a-waiting outside the gates, with about twenty musket balls aimed for his heart. Here's the letter, sir." The man explained, extending his arm. In his hand he held a parchment envelope bearing a red wax seal.

"Thank you." West responded simply. The hand, understanding that he'd been dismissed, withdrew.

Upon careful examination of the seal, West discovered it to be British. With a cry of surprise and joy, he tore open the envelope and read the sheet within.

Commanding Officer
American Station at Santa Eugenia
March 30, 1802

My Dear Sir,

Allow me to congratulate you on your astounding feat of war, the capture of the Santa Eugenia Shore Battery. My name is Joseph Lawford, His Majesty's Ambassador to Spain, stationed in Madrid. I am currently residing in Bilbao, however, relatively close to your own location. Political tension is building between the Royal British Government and His Spanish Majesty. I suspect there will soon be war, and so I fear for my own safety, and that of my family.

Before I ask of you, dear American ally, the favor I so desperately require, allow me to provide intelligence in the sincere hope that it will aid your cause. Two battalions of Spanish Army troops are preparing to leave Bilbao for your location. News of your conquest has traveled rapidly, and the Spanish are suitably furious. They intend to attempt to retake the fort very soon, though regretfully I am not privy to when. They bring with them twelve artillery pieces, however, and shall probably reach the fort by the fourteenth of March.

And now, my dear sir, allow me to request of you a minor favor. As I earlier stated, military action is close between my nation and Spain. I fear that, if I do not flee the country very soon indeed, I or my family may be endangered. Thus I beseech you, sir, as an ally and a gentleman, accept my wife and daughter into your charge and conduct them with you to the nearest friendly port. I would not ask it unless it were of the gravest importance, and I can only hope you shall accept. My messenger has been instructed to await your reply.

I am certain that His Most Brittanic Majesty would offer his military assistance to your cause in such a case as this, but I regret to say that no troops or ships are within suitable range. Whether or no you undertake the task I have requested, I wish you the best in the remainder of your voyage.

Your Friend and Ally,
Sir Joseph Lawford, K.C. B.

Despite the disappointment West felt at the absence of a promise for military aid, it was refreshing to have friendly contact once more. For so long, he'd been alone, unable to confide in even the able-minded Tallis. For though West thought of him as an equal, strict naval tradition forbid any semblance of close friendship between officers of differing rank or position. It was a matter of respect, courtesy, and formality, and West would not cross such a line.

The ambassador's request was a separate matter entirely. Two women aboard a ship of war? It was unheard of, absurd! They would be underfoot the entire home voyage, to say nothing of the eventual retreat from the fort. What if they were injured, or even killed? And during a battle? What would he do with two women in the heat of action, splinters impaling foremast hands and round shot coming in through the side? No, it was impossible. They would be nothing but a liability for he and his crew.

On the other hand, the ambassador had been very generous in his letter with provisions for the safety of *Perseverance*'s crew. It was quite obvious that the entire reason for such an awkward message was to ensure the well-being of the man's family, but the fact that attempts were made to show genuine concern spoke volumes about the fellow. It was clear that these two women were extremely important to this desperate chap, and that something would have to be done about it.

West wasn't quite certain why; perhaps it was because he had no family of his own, or perhaps his attachment to Great Britain bore some influence, but he found himself scrawling out a reply to the affirmative, signing and sealing it, and passing it to a mate to give to the messenger. It was done; the two would be arriving shortly.

In the meantime, West had quite a lot with which to occupy his mind. Still more mortar shells had to be forged, and further defenses erected for the arrival of the Spanish army. But by the fall of dusk, when West slipped into a blissfully dreamless sleep, he had forgotten all his cares regarding the women.

CHAPTER 13

Slowly the sun pulled itself free of the imprisoning horizon, racing into the Ria de Arosa from the broad Continent and falling lazily down on the stone battlements set high upon the cliffs. It ran across the shoreline, slipping and trickling through the trees and down the rocky slopes to the water, where *Perseverance* swung to her anchor. Another day had dawned, and another chance for West and his crew.

The door seemed to shudder frantically in the dim morning light, and West wondered if he was witnessing an earthquake. He had never seen one before, and it was something about which he was mildly curious. He rubbed the sleep out of his eyes, suddenly interested, and then felt his heart sink as he came to full consciousness. Someone was pounding on the door, and evidently had been for some time.

"Enter!" West called. The door swung wide.

"News, sir," said Tallis, entering and removing his hat. "From the gunners' mate. They've got the powder and the fuses right."

"I'll come." West announced, leaping from his bed, all yesterday's despair behind him. The shipyards, the objective towards which he had been striving for months, lay finally within striking distance. Soon he would be happily sailing back for Marblehead in Boston, and he'd see his beloved America again.

But for now, work.

Running to his sea chest (and feeling completely ridiculous all the while), West donned his uniform and snatched up his hat as he rushed out into the fort commons. The sea air was cool and refreshing, laden with the evaporated dew of early morning. On the channel side of the fort, activity was centered around the mortar station. Looking cool and perfectly dignified (the captain had not forgotten his obligation to appear imperturbable), West strode into the center of the group, which parted to accept him. A gunners' mate, apparently one who had been working through the night, approached him, grinning like a child. Stiles was the man's name, West recalled.

"We've got it, sir, I do believe," Stiles announced, appearing giddy and energetic despite a long night of hard work. "In a moment we'll be ready to fire." He set to work measuring and cutting the fuses for the first shell, double checking each step as he went along. After a moment of silence, he stood up, holding the shell in his hands. "Done, sir."

"Excellent work, Mr. Stiles. You may fire at will." West ordered, nearly as excited himself. The success of this shot would mean an earlier departure from Spain. He only hoped it didn't falter.

Tentatively, Stiles laid match to the outer fuse and dropped the mortar shell into the great barrel. West was handed a spyglass from somewhere behind him. He held it at the ready, prepared to watch the shell explode. There was a sudden, hollow *thunk* as the mortar went off. West raised the glass.

The shell sped rapidly away, upward into the atmosphere, and then suddenly down into the valley separating the cliffs of the fort and the lowlands of the shipyards. In between the channel lay crisply and peacefully. Suddenly there was en explosion—inaudible from West's distance—directly over the shipyards. The mortar shell had found its mark, raining burning bits of shrapnel down on the position below. West shuddered at the memory of similar shells tearing through the rigging aboard the old *Nova*.

"Well done, Mr. Stiles!" he nearly shouted, relieved. "Keep it up, now! I want two hundred new shells forged by noon, exactly to your specifications. Don't let up on them for a moment."

"Aye aye, sir!" Stiles beamed, exhilarated by this praise from the captain.

West smiled wryly as he meandered contentedly away. He could imagine the scene at the Spanish shipyards right now; confusion as men struggled to comprehend what was happening, running to put out what few minor fires had been ignited by the first explosion. It would not be so for long, however. Soon, once Stiles had both mortars working a steady rhythm, the Spaniards would find themselves pounded relentlessly, entirely helpless to put an end to the attack. By the time a message runner could be dispatched to Bilbao, it would all be over, and the entire shipyards would be ablaze. West pondered the two scenes; ironic that here at Santa Eugenia, there was little sense of immediate danger, and firing proceeded at a leisurely pace, while all would soon be chaos at the opposite end of the channel. He was finally able to carry out his orders directly, which imbued him with a sense of satisfaction. It was only a matter of time now.

Forcing back a relieved smile, West checked his pocketwatch and paused to eat a meager breakfast of steak and eggs, rapidly prepared by Sway. Once that was out of the way, he returned to the mortar station for an update on progress. The firing was not yet ready to begin in earnest; final preparations would take another hour. In the meantime, however, balls were forged in the armory and powder moved into convenient position.

Across the fort from West, just above the gate, a lookout shouted for attention. West responded coolly.

"What do you see?" he rasped.

"Carriage drawn by two horses one quarter mile down the road! She's bearing a white banner, sir!" the sentry answered. Those would be the ambassador's relations.

"Very good. Hold your fire, but do not yet allow admittance." West ordered, striding briskly in that direction to affect a welcome.

The chaise carriage lurched to a halt outside the fort's gate only moments later. West and a small armed contingency of marines awaited the emergence of its passengers. If it was a deception, they would all know in a moment.

The chaise door opened, and the driver, another Spaniard, handed down a charming, fair-skinned woman of about fifty with brown eyes and graying hair. She wore a long plain dress with yellow trim, her curls of hair hanging loosely about her shoulders. This would be the ambassador's wife.

Next came his daughter. As she stepped delicately onto the running board of the carriage, she made brief eye contact with West. She was strikingly beautiful; her well-proportioned figure blended easily with her face and hair, giving a surprising impression of grace scarcely met with in such times. She, too, was handed down out of the chaise, and the driver tipped his hat and resumed his seat. West stepped forward, touching his hat and then folding his arms behind his back.

"It is with great pleasure, madam and mademoiselle, that I welcome you to the Santa Eugenia shore battery, currently under American control. Captain Lowell J. West, at your service," said he, bowing low. The elder of the two women stepped forward at this, offering her hand. He kissed it.

"Thank you very much indeed, Captain West," she responded, smiling pleasantly. "My daughter and I are extremely grateful of your hospitality. The Ambassador sends his regards. Oh, well I have forgotten my manners! I am Jane Lawford, and this is my daughter, Emily. Pleased to make your acquaintance." Both women curtsied, and West bowed again.

"Delighted, ma'am, delighted. Would you care to accompany me through the gates?" he replied, offering her his arm. She took it, and her daughter was escorted in by the marine sergeant.

West quartered the two women in the secondary bedrooms of the main command building, where the commandant of the fort would have housed his family. Their baggage was unloaded from the carriage, which departed briskly, and carried up to the rooms by the boatswain's mates. West arranged for Tallis to offer the guests a tour of the fort while he attended to the mortars and the other final preparations for the eventual evacuation of the fort.

When West had returned to the mortar position, firing was almost ready to begin. Shells were stacked neatly nearby, fire buckets held at the ready, and the aim perfected. All that was required was the order.

West picked up his glass and studied the shipyards once again. That was his objective, and this was his opportunity to strike. He shut the telescope.

"Fire."

"Aye aye, sir."

"Ranging shots first, you understand, and then I want a steady rhythm. Pound them until there is nothing left."

"Aye, sir."

"Very good."

The first few shots were stilted and uneven, but gradually a pattern assembled itself, and soon mortar shells were exploding over the shipyards with a deadly accuracy every few seconds. For West and for the Spanish North Atlantic Squadron, it was the beginning of the end. From here all roads led to one of two destinations: utter destruction for the Spanish navy and victory for West, or precisely the reverse. There was no third option, no alternate path. Victory, or defeat, would be complete.

Lunch was served out to the fort's company presently, and the watch was changed regularly, as aboardships. Throughout the afternoon, the firing continued at a steady pace, and Tallis entertained the womenfolk. There was no reason for anxiousness, and yet West was hopelessly tense. He had the sudden, disconcerting feeling that all was not well, that something beyond his control would occur at any moment. His heart rate increased and the hair at the back of his neck stood on end. Try as he might, he could not relax, and was nearly overcome by the urge to flee.

Dinner was not enjoyable at all. West was obliged to eat with the two guests, and to discuss such lubber subjects as politics, culture, and cuisine. Day faded into dusk, and dusk to night. There was no moon, so all was pitch black quite suddenly. Now flashes accompanied the customary explosions as mortars were launched from the fort, and the countryside below was lit regularly with an angry red light, like some variety of hellish lightning. It was clear that many of the secondary buildings and ship frameworks at the shipyards had caught fire already, but the main complex had yet to burn. It would still be several hours before the deed was done.

At eleven 'o clock, West was attempting to take his mind off of his heavy, foreboding feeling by trying his luck at a hand of whist with his officers. His spirits were lifted momentarily; he seemed to be on a winning streak. Suddenly, Bellows, a topman, threw himself into the room with a great shout.

"Captain, sir! You'd better come, sir. Harland, the watch, can hear marching drums!"

West was on his feet in an instant, the card game forgotten. He donned his greatcloak and emerged from the warmth of his chambers into the cold Spanish night. When he reached the gate, the watch was awaiting him.

"Take my night-glass, sir. Can't see much, but there may be something there," said Harland, proffering a telescope.

"Silence fore and aft!" roared West, bending his senses forward into the night wind. It was thin, coming only in snatches now and again, but there was a definite drumbeat riding through the air. Gradually it intensified, recognizable as a marching cadence. He raised the night-glass, seeing nothing at first. But then vague shapes appeared against the forest ahead: white uniforms. The Spanish army had arrived, early, and would be knocking on his door in half an hour's time.

Shutting the glass with a curse, West turned on his heel and sprang into action, the blood rushing to his head and a familiar battle-cunning propelling his mind forward. The mortaring could not move any more rapidly, so it would take another two or three hours to destroy the shipyards, and West was determined not to depart without having accomplished this task. Defenses would have to be speedily rigged, the women gotten to safety. Oh, why had he ever agreed to bear the Ambassador's burden? No matter; something would have to be done.

"Mr. Tallis!" he called, striding rapidly back towards his office to retrieve his sword-belt and pistols.

"Sir?" came the response from the inky darkness. The lieutenant appeared faithfully beside him.

"Call all hands and turn out the full marine guard. Arm the men, but quietly now. We mustn't let the enemy know we are expecting them. Summon the crew of the cutter, and have Mr. Caswell escort the Ambassador's relations back to the ship. Once aboard, he should send back the boat, see the womenfolk safely berthed in the wardroom, and return ashore directly. Is that clear?"

"Quite clear, sir."

"Good. On top of that, you are to relay these instructions to Mr. Nettleton: Stand ready to make sail rapidly, and when the mortars cease their belching, set as much canvas as she will carry and bring the ship round to the point below the fort."

"Right, sir."

"Excellent. That is all, Mr. Tallis."

"Aye aye, sir."

As the first lieutenant disappeared into the night, West realized that he had more to worry about than just soldiers. The Spanish were probably fairly certain that the *Perseverance* still lurked nearby.

There would also be a ship.

CHAPTER 14

Inside the fort, all was chaos as the Spanish army approached. The steady *rap-tap* of the relentless snare drums was now audible over all the battle preparations, and time was known to be short.

Men bolted to and fro as final adjustments were made; weapons gathered, bulkheads struck, and marines assembled. The plague patients had been brought inside once more, having shown little sign of worsening since the day before. They were now being transferred back aboard the ship by the cutter, to be quartered in the cramped cockpit once more.

West had assembled the ship's company into their two respective watches, and the starboard one he stationed well within the gates. He arranged the remainder of his forces on either side of the road outside the walls, and then waited, the measured *rom—rom—rom* of the mortars punctuating the silence, and the even time of the approaching snare drums setting his nerves on edge. It was to be a hard-fought battle, and he was uncertain which side would win.

He could see the Spaniards very clearly now; four long columns led by three officers on horseback, and he did not require a telescope to tell that it was at least a full battalion. The fighting would be bloody, and it would begin soon.

Now the enemy was only a quarter mile away and closing fast. West gave a nod to the sergeant of marines, and looked down the road at his seamen, arrayed symmetrically on either side of it.

The sergeant nodded in reply, and waited another three minutes, then yelled, "Fire!" at the top of his lungs. Instantly, a crashing volley of musket-fire exploded from the wall above the fort's gate. A few Spanish soldiers were brought down by the attack, but the columns advanced still. A second volley rang out, and finally the crucial order was barked by one of the mounted men. The Spaniards came to a neat halt, and the first row dropped to their knees to return fire.

Just as the order to fire was about to be given, West shouted a command of his own.

"Charge!" he hollered, emerging from the forest beside the road with his pistols brought to bear. A hundred sailors and marines took up the yell from their positions at the enemy's flanks, and all at once the entire force came upon the unwelcome battalion from both sides, causing utter confusion among the Spanish officers and men. For a moment the Americans had the clear upper hand, but then the enemy realized that they were up against an inferior force. Just as they began to push their attackers back from the road, West barked an order, and all of his forces disappeared instantly into the forest from whence they came. There were a few seconds of bewilderment among the Spanish, and then the land-facing carronade in the fort's gate opened up on them with grape shot, firing three times before anyone knew what had occurred. It was the same plan he had used to take the fort, and it worked equally well in its defense.

By this time, West was certain that the Spanish officers had deduced his strategy: keep up the fighting from as many fronts as possible in order to appear to have the greater force. It was thus time to change tactics.

"Now!" he barked at the marine sergeant quite suddenly, and all at once the carronading ceased. This time the Spaniards recovered quickly, charging the fort walls with all the speed and ferocity they could muster. In reply, the gates were opened and the sailors and marines within poured outwards onto the road, clashing with the enemy just outside the walls. This afforded West's personnel time enough to re-enter the fort, and then to order the other American forces to do the same. Soon, all of the *Perseverance*'s company stood within the fort's confines once again, firing down upon the unlucky Spaniards below and cutting their grappling lines as they were hurled up.

West was satisfied that the first portion of the battle had occurred precisely as planned. Already the enemy was well shaken-up, and the Americans had a position superior to their own. The fort could probably be held until the shipyards was destroyed through use of the mortars, and then a careful, calculated retreat could begin.

Outside the walls, the sounds of battle could be constantly heard; scattered gunfire, screams, and the boom of the gate carronade as it raked the opposing force. The fighting would be fierce for several hours, and by then, hopefully, West could withdraw. If the fort could not be held long enough, however, it was uncertain what would occur.

West strode over to the mortar positions quite casually, trying desperately to ignore the acrid black battle smoke rising from the gates behind him and the urge to plunge recklessly into action. He addressed the gunner's mates as he neared the mortar tubes themselves.

"What progress?"

"Well, sir, looks from 'ere like we've got them on the run. At first, pretty much everything we done set aflame was put out real quick. By now, though, I thinks we caused a near-total retreat. It's only a matter 'o time until the complex itself is destroyed," reported the senior man there, smiling grimly.

"You're certain the damage affected will be permanent?"

"Aye, sir. You can take my night-glass if you want to be real sure." He proffered the instrument. West took it and raised it slowly, finding the shipyards easily in the darkness of night.

Between the mortar bursts, he could indeed tell that most of the buildings that made up the collective shipbuilding facility were on fire and burning furiously, and there did not seem to be any organized effort to put out the blaze. Yes, what once was touched by flame tonight would be impossible to repair, thought West, relieved at the effect of his attack. If he could just hold the fort a little longer...

Unable to resist, the captain reloaded his pistols, retrieved a musket from the arms locker, and joined his men at the fort's wall, shooting into the disorganized mass of Spanish soldiers that pressed in against the base of the stone battlement. Balls howled over his head and screamed past very close by, catching a few of his men in their upper extremities and requiring a visit to the surgeon, who lay down in the sick ward awaiting potential patients.

The fighting continued in earnest for another hour before West realized that the Spaniards had withdrawn the main body of their force to the road beyond, leaving only a small contingent of men to fire up at the fort. That could mean only one thing: another organized assault, this time to gain entry to the fort.

By now tired and disheveled, West did not relish the idea of fending off another frontal attack. He withdrew from the line and sprinted back to the mortars, leaving behind him the raging din of battle.

"What progress?" he asked again, presenting quite a spectacle standing there before the gunners, his hat nearly falling off, his hair protruding from under it, and two smoking pistols clutched desperately in his hands. Sweat poured down his forehead, nearly blinding him as he awaited the reply.

"We believe the headquarters to be aflame now, sir," answered Caswell, who West had not noticed until he spoke. Evidently, he had taken a lead ball in the arm and had retreated to this secondary front of battle.

"How much time?" At this question there was a moment's pause; finally the lieutenant spoke up again.

"At least another hour, sir, if not more."

Another hour! How was that going to be possible? West drew his watch from his pocket and glanced at it—already one in the morning. The fighting had begun at a little past eleven; three hours. Could the fort be held for another hour? Could he and his crew safely withdraw to the ship once that hour had finished? It was preposterous!

Feeling more than a little weak at the knees, West turned slowly to face the gate again—and was greeted by a sight that brought his worst fears vividly to life. As he watched, the gate was rent from its hinges with a monstrous roar—the work of an artillery piece, no doubt—and Spanish officers and men poured into the fort commons, pistols cracking and muskets vomiting death in all directions. A ball whistled through the air just inches from his ear, and then the artillery spoke again. The battle had become truly desperate, and for the first time he felt completely overcome by a fear for his life. Swallowing all emotion, he plunged into the thick of it, wiping the sweat from his brow as he drew his cutlass.

He found his first opponent only a few hundred yards away, an officer taking up a rallying cry to urge his men onwards. With a savage shout of his own, West was upon the man, their blades clashing at the same instant that the enemy cannon let loose for the third time. The noise shook the Spaniard ever so slightly, allowing West a precious fraction of a second to strike again. The poor man spotted the blow as it fell, but was too late to stop it.

Stepping over the corpse, West forged ahead into the crowd, drawing both his pistols and pointing them randomly into the huge, heaving mass of enemy soldiers that surged inwards from the gate. Two men fell, but a dozen more rose in their place. West knew the fort could not be long held. Casualties would be heavy.

And still they battled on, driven madly by the familiar rush of unbridled fury associated with war. For hours, it seemed, men fell on both sides as the Americans struggled to push the Spaniards back from their already advanced position. Gradually the line gave way, only to lurch forward again in another moment, propelled on the blades of five hundred Spanish swords. Desperate hand-to-hand combat, booming artillery, and the thunderous, regular roar emulated by the mortars filled the air with intoxicating sights and sounds as still each man became more fierce.

And then the mortars stopped.

West was suddenly deaf to all that was happening around him, his vision narrowing to focus on Caswell and the gunner's mates: one of them waved victoriously. It was over. The shipyards was no more.

West, now knowing precisely what had to be done, sprang away from the body of another fallen enemy and, with a quick motion of his arm, signaled a half dozen seamen to follow. This determined band approached the outer wall of the shore battery—the guns themselves.

"Strike the tackles and pitch them into the sea!" West cried, motioning again to the huge cannons. "Shake a leg about it, then!"

Instantly the men set to work, removing the preventive braces, shattering the safety tackles, and then, heaving with all their might, toppling the huge iron monsters over the cliff and into the Atlantic beyond, where they could not possibly be used to fire upon the *Perseverance* as she ran out to sea.

Perfectly on cue, West caught a bit of white out of the corner of his eye—*Perseverance*'s topsails. She was a beautiful sight, adjusting her trim and preparing to heave-to in order to embark the rest of her crew. Her captain felt a sudden proud thrill at beholding his ship again for so long—her flowing, familiar lines, low man-of-war cut, and lofty sails filling him with an intense sense of relief. He felt that if only he could make it to stand upon her deck again that he would survive, that the fighting would be over.

Seeing the last forty-two pounder satisfactorily over the cliff, West called a hasty retreat to his men, rushing for the previously rigged escape ropes that led up the fort's wall and into the dense forests. Taking one in his hands as other shipmates and marines did the same, he heaved himself onto the stone face and then climbed to the top of the wall, leaping off into nothingness and landing uncomfortably along the fringe of the woods. Jumping rapidly to his feet, he ran like the devil under the cover of branches, and then kept running until he found the trail that led down the cliff to the sea. His men were all around him, racing along in front of and behind their captain to reach the ship. Back inside the fort walls, he knew, a rearguard of marines ensured a safe retreat and then, once all had made it, turned and bolted themselves, setting match to the kerosene-soaked escape ropes as the last man was over. It was an ingenious retreat plan, devised primarily by Tallis and West as the Spanish army approached earlier that night.

Now, somewhere down ahead of him at the shore, West could see his sloop's quarterboat taking on the first crew members for the transfer to the ship. Once she was full to the brim, she spun neatly to join *Perseverance* out in the channel, and the ship's cutter pulled into her place and immediately began to fill.

Seeing that the cutter was about to row out from the dock just as he approached it, West increased his pace still further, making a final leap into the sternsheets of the little boat as fast as a ball from a musket. He landed awkwardly, and immediately scrambled to regain composure. That was it. He'd made it.

Watching the oars descend into the sea as if from a great distance, West was aware that the boat was finally pulling hard away from the unfriendly Spanish shore. He was altogether glad to be gone, and happy to be rocking gently with the waves again.

He surveyed himself. As usual, his uniform had been cut to pieces during the action, and there was blood spattered all over him. He was suddenly aware of a sharp pain in his left side, and reached down to discover that he had been stabbed twice there, though not very seriously. The wounds would be a bother to deal with, but not a threat to his life. Then the command came, "Up oars!", and the cutter was neatly lain alongside the ship.

West was first on deck from his boat, ascending the side awkwardly because of the rolling sea and the pain in his torso. He was piped aboard as usual, the spotless sideboys manning the rail to the twittering of the boatswain's pipes. He exchanged a crisp salute with Nettleton, who stood in the captain's usual place on the quarterdeck.

"Welcome aboard, sir," said the nervous third lieutenant, anxious to hear his superior's reaction to his handling of the ship.

"Thank you, Mr. Nettleton. Well done, then," West replied, taking the younger man's place aft of the wheel and next to the binnacle. He nodded at the helmsman at the wheel and the quartermaster at the con, adding, "Stand by to wear the ship once all hands have returned aboard."

Upon the very summit of the cliff near the fort, West could just make out the rearguard of marines fleeing for their lives, firing behind them at the advancing enemy troops at intervals. The last boatload of sailors was now alongside, and it would only take another trip to pick the last marines off the shore.

"Mr. Tallis, sway up the gig and cutter and send the quarterboat ashore for the rearguard," West barked at the haggard first lieutenant, slightly relieved to be back in control of the situation. He could not completely relax until they were well out to sea, and his anxiousness for the last contingent of marines was beyond words.

"Aye aye, sir," Tallis responded, catching a master's mate as he ran past and relaying the order. In moments all the boats were back aboard save the last one, now lightly aground against the base of the promontory and awaiting its passengers. Finally the last American soldiers in Spain came cascading down to the little dock, piling hurriedly into the boat as a few despondent shots rang out from the

Spaniards. The last man was aboard, and the quarterboat was pulling for the *Perseverance* with all her might.

"Boat alongside, sir, and all hands and marines accounted for," reported Tallis after another long moment.

"Excellent, Mr. Tallis. You may sway up the quarterboat and call all hands."

"Aye aye, sir. Johnson, man those tackles and get the last boat in. All hands! All hands!"

The boatswain's pipes trilled their call, and there was a sudden scattered pounding of feet and a rough gathering of men on deck.

"Ship's company assembled, sir."

"Thank you, Mr. Tallis. Lay aloft! Set her t'gallants to the wind, lads!"

The crew raced into the rigging at a record pace, skipping along the yards and flying canvas as though they had never gone ashore.

"Haul the main, now! Sheet home!" ordered West as the sails filled lightly, flapped once, and then ballooned out ahead again. "Starboard trim! Port trim!"

Slowly, *Perseverance* gathered headway, heeling over slightly on the starboard tack and dropping the larboard broadside lower in the water. The water creamed up under the bows and then crashed over them as she took a wave in the teeth, recovering smartly and dropping off to round a sudden bend in the channel. It was very good to be at sea again.

High atop the cliff, musket volleys crackled out from the Spanish battalion that now held the shore battery, the shot falling harmlessly through the sloop's rigging.

West, peering into the darkness over the bowsprit, saw the earth on both flanks of the Ria de Arosa fall away: the great, stormy Atlantic, stretching out triumphantly past the horizon to America, to Boston. He felt a sudden exhilaration at the majestic sight coupled with the singing of the wind in the rigging and the great creaking of the deck beneath his feet. And then the banks fell away entirely, and he was out of the damned little channel forever.

Now the Spaniards had swayed an artillery piece up to the gun fittings of the shore battery and were firing on his retreating ship dispiritedly, but the shot fell several hundred yards short. He was free.

After another moment on deck to assure himself that all was well with the vessel and crew, West turned on his heel to enter his aft cabin for some much-overdue rest.

"Sail ho!" cried the foretopmast lookout quite suddenly, causing West to look round in alarm.

"Where away?" he called back, hoping against hope that she was an ally. His heart began to pound in his chest again, and adrenaline flooded his body.

"One point abaft the port beam, sir, and running hard for us!"

West glanced over his shoulder down the *Perseverance*'s larboard side. Sure enough, a tiny white fleck appeared just on the horizon and sailing hard. With a glass her royals could just be seen: without doubt a man-of-war.

"What do you make of her?" he called to the lookout at the main crosstrees.

"Spanish two-decker, probably an eighty-four, sir, and bearing on a course to cut across ours in about two miles. All possible sail set aboard her, sir."

A ship of the line! With forty-one guns a side and two bow chasers, this was a force that virtually no American ship could deal with. West would have no choice but to alter course and run from her. He could not, therefore, sail for the American continent, but had better drive hard for England.

"Course nor'nor'east, Mr. Bowles," West ordered, addressing the quartermaster. "Mr. Tallis, set full sail with no reefs and all stays'ls. We may be able to outrun her yet."

Perseverance went hard about and settled easily onto her new course, lurching healthily forward as the extra canvas was borne, but it was clear that the enemy ship was sailing two miles to her one. It would not be long before they opened up with the bow chaser, and then the broadside. With that kind of firepower, it was doubtful that the little sloop could stand as many as three broadsides. The colors would have to be struck before the first was let loose.

As the minutes ebbed slowly away and the pursuing ship grew rapidly closer to *Perseverance*'s stern, a feeling of urgency darkened West's mind the likes of which he had never felt before. This was it, and unless he could think of a workable solution very soon, his ship and probably his body would be on their way to either the bottom of the Atlantic or a nearby Spanish prison.

"Mr. Tallis," he called. "Throw the stores overboard."

"All of them sir?"

"All of them."

"Aye aye, sir."

There was a long pause as orders were passed down the line, but soon all of the foodstuffs and galley equipment was up from below and down over the side. West looked behind him, understanding his position. He turned again to the first lieutenant.

"Get all but one cask of water pumped out."

"Aye aye, sir." Soon, the bilge pumps were on deck, and almost every drop of the *Perseverance*'s precious fresh water dribbled into the sea. Still the Spanish ship gained on them.

"Powder and shot, Mr. Tallis."

"Aye aye, sir."

A tiny stab of orange light appeared somewhere astern of the American ship, followed closely by the report of a cannon and a jet of water off the starboard side. A ranging shot with the bow-chaser. The next one crashed through one of the stern windows, pierced the bulkhead opposing it, and then hit the mizzenmast dejectedly and fell to the deck, rolling about with the ship's motion until a midshipman heaved it over the side. Twenty-four pound shot; it was going to be a hammering for certain. Soon there was a steady rate of fire from the two-decker, howling through the rigging or splintering the stern of the smaller ship. The two vessels were no more than a quarter mile apart now, and the Spaniard loomed large off *Perseverance*'s stern. Just a little closer, West knew, and then the broadside would be presented and fired. Another ball whipped through the main topgallantsail.

Gunpowder and shot were far more precious than water aboard any American vessel because of their incredible scarcity, and now West's ship was pouring them overboard like human excrement.

"Cast loose the gun carriages and prepare to throw all the carronades overboard as well," West ordered. This was it.

"Aye aye, sir," Tallis responded, looking as anxious as his captain as the last of the shot went into the sea.

West looked thoughtfully back at the fast-approaching enemy ship. The sloop under his feet had increased her speed considerably in this newly-lightened state; perhaps it would be enough to keep the big Spaniard from closing the rest of the distance. For a moment, it seemed as though she continued to gain, and West was about to have the guns heaved overboard—but then it became apparent that the enemy ship was dropping behind. Slowly, ever so slowly, her stern lanterns dropped away and her great bows receded, so West ordered the carronades lashed down as they had been before. As he did so, the entire ship's company gave a great yell of joy, and he began to breathe again.

"Silence fore and aft!" he roared, but it was too late. Someone had shouted, "Three cheers for the Captain!" and the crew had taken up the cry.

"Hip-hip—hooray! Hip-hip—hooray! Hip-hip—hooray!"

West smiled openly as he tried to extinguish the noise, his heart soaring at the knowledge that the long, hard battle was finally won. He glanced aft one more time.

The now-distant Spanish ship of the line came to the wind at just that moment, presenting her starboard side. Suddenly the ship vanished as smoke sprang from her side: a parting broadside. The shot fell short by nearly half a cable's length, and the huge, ponderous vessel heaved herself about once more, letting her stern show in retreat. A final orange stab lit up the not-quite-so-dark air—morning was nearly upon them—and West watched for the fall of this last, disdainful shot.

He did not see it, for at that instant his left shoulder exploded in intense pain and he was spun forcefully around, hitting the quarterdeck hard on his right side.

He saw the concerned faces of the crew, saw Tallis bend over him calling for the ship's surgeon, and then his vision faded to black.

CHAPTER 15

There was no creaking.

It was completely silent, something to which a sailor of many years was not accustomed by any stretch of the imagination. There was no rocking, no gentle swell. The footfalls over his head, on the quarterdeck, that signaled the beginning of a new day. The bell did not clang out the changing of the watch. He was not at sea.

Where was he?

Lowell West opened his eyes, looking cautiously round him. Rather than the stark bulkheads of *Perseverance*'s aft cabin, he was greeted by the bright, well-appointed interior of a large bedroom, obviously at least two stories above ground level. At his right, there was a large mirror: his reflection was appalling. His face was rough, unshaven, and pale, his cheeks hallow and thin, and his eyes deep set and dark. To make matters worse, there was a cumbersome bandage draped around his left shoulder, and his arm hung in a sling. As he attempted to move it, he felt a surge of hot pain, so he tried no more. Looking out his window he saw—*what was it he saw?* A city street, certainly; but not Boston, New York, or Philadelphia. He had seen it before, years ago—London?

The door opened and a short, rather portly gentleman entered, holding a snifter of brandy. He stopped short at the sight of West's upright form.

"Ah! Awake, after all this time! Splendid to see, I say!" said the fellow, obviously an American. He spoke with what the English referred to as a "colonial drawl".

"How long have I been unconscious?" West asked tentatively, a frown on his face.

"Oh, I dare say almost six weeks by now. For a little while there, we thought we'd lost you—but you came around, didn't you, then, by jove!"

"Where am I?"

"Ah, forgive me, Captain West. I have not covered the details. I shall be brief. You wish me to begin at your arrival, I'll wager?"

"If you please."

"Well, as I say, around six weeks ago your ship comes sailing into Spithead triumphantly, but not paying a moment's attention to all the hubbub they aroused. Man called Tallin—Tallies?"

"Tallis," corrected West.

"Forgive me. Tallis—keeps asking for the best doctors in England. Well, they finally got some pinch-a-penny physician down there, and this fellow takes him into your cabin to see you. You were very bad at first—ship's surgeon hadn't been able to remove all the lead."

"Lead?"

"Why yes, my dear boy, you were struck on the shoulder by cannon shot! The way the naval men tell it, your officers and all, they say that some Spanish ship fired a stern chaser of grape shot at you, and you were the only one hit. This Tallies—Tallis fellow takes command and sails you right up here for medical help. When you were seen to be improving, about three weeks ago, they had you moved here—The American Embassy, in London. I'm Mr. John Edward, by the bye."

"And they say I'm on the up and up?"

"Indeed! Quite a good thing, too, with the whole damned world talking about you."

West felt a sudden stab of fear. Had he done entirely wrong? Made too much commotion and caused a war with Spain? Was he to be court-martialed?

"I beg—I beg your pardon?" he finally asked nervously.

"Why didn't you know? You're the toast of the town, my lad! Even before you pulled in, everybody heard about this 'mystery ship' that's dumbfounded the Spanish. Eventually we got wind of a name—*Perseverance*, if I'm not mistaken—but everyone was confused about your size. The Spaniards insisted they were being tormented by a huge ship of the line, more than a hundred guns, sinking ships, laying waste to towns, all that. Turned out to be but rumor, you know—but when you arrived here, everyone was talking! I dare say your first lieutenant's report was published in every naval gazette in the Western world, and it's almost better than fiction! Prizes taken, an entire fort held for a week, a shipyards leveled, the brilliant strategy behind it all. Rescued the English Ambassador's relatives, too, if I'm not mistaken. All very dashing. It's been called the naval exploit of the year—are you quite all right, sir?"

West's head was swimming—exploit of the year? And all this time he was worried about court-martial! It had come off as a success! It was inconceivable—all this celebration, the press, gossip. He was known now, famous, *successful*! It was more than he could have dreamed!

"Yes—yes, thank you, I am well," he stammered, disbelieving all of this. It was too much information at once—he must slow down.

Just then, the door burst open, and Tallis came rushing in, holding his hat under his arm and wearing the uniform of a Master and Commander.

"Captain West, sir! Capital to see you awake, sir! I'm—we're all so relieved. The ship's company has been asking about you constantly, not to mention the papers. I'm glad to see you, sir." Tears welled up in his eyes, but he forced them down and went on. "We've done it, sir, we've done it! Up to this moment, I was worried you might not pull through, but you have. And I've got a promotion! You have, too, sir, you have too!"

"A promotion!" West's eyes widened as he attempted to sort out his emotions. Tallis lunged forward, a recent edition of the *Boston Naval Chronicle* under his arm.

Sure enough, there he was: first on the list of Promotions, Ship Arrivals and Departures. "Commander Lowell J. West, recently of *Perseverance*, promoted Captain." It was that simple.

"And these arrived for you just a day ago with the rest of the mail," said the ambassador. He produced a thick parchment envelope, sealed with the familiar Navy crest, and West tore it open eagerly, giddy as a schoolboy at this new excitement. He read the enclosed notice.

Cmdr. Lowell West
U.S.S. Perseverance, Spithead
London, England

U.S. War Department
Division of the Navy
Hartt Yards, Boston

Dear Sir,

The Navy Department and the Government of the United States of America do hereby Recognize and Commend your heroic actions against the Enemy in command of the Sloop of War <u>Perseverance</u>*. Hearty Congratulations are in order.*

Upon receipt of this document, you are hereby requested and required to accept promotion to the Honorable Rank of Captain, U. S. Navy, and to take Immediate Command of the Frigate U.S.S. <u>United States</u>*, currently at Plymouth.*

Upon completion of these Orders, you are directed to return to West Indies Station in Jamaica for victuals and supplies, pending further Orders.

Your ob't servant,
Commodore Charles Reid

There it was, in plain black and white. He was being entrusted with one of the most coveted commands in the entire Navy—a sister ship of the *Constitution*. That must also mean that Estleman's squadron had been removed from station due to the success of his mission. Captain Wilson must be proud, thought West. He would probably be detailed to the West Indies Squadron for the time being, and then sent back to Marblehead now and then for further orders and updates.

But for now, there was much to do.

One week later, dressed in the double-epauletted uniform of a post Captain, West finally emerged onto the streets of London, his recovery nearly complete. His wound was closed now, and he could move his arm without much pain. According to the doctor, if he used it as little as possible for the next several weeks, he should have no future indication of the wound save his nasty scar.

He checked his watch. Half past eleven; his first appointment was for lunch at Admiralty with the First Lord. He was extremely nervous about the encounter, but he could not refuse the invitation.

As the chaise coach dropped him off at Whitehall Steps, he felt a surge of pride at his heritage and his affiliation—national pride both for the United States and his native England. He was happy to have served both during his last commission.

It was drizzling dimly as he pulled his boatcloak about him and trod roughly across the wet cobblestones to the foot of the steps. He ran purposefully up to the wide door, touching his hat to the sentry as he entered.

Inside, the vast marble floor was engraved with the image of a compass, and the ceilings were painted lavishly with scenes of famous naval battles reaching back into the depths of the Renaissance. A uniformed midshipman took his coat and pointed the way to his meeting for him. Ahead, he spotted the grand marble staircase, and began to ascend. At the top, he was directed through a doorway on the left by another young officer, and then he found himself standing in the entranceway of a great ballroom.

It was decorated in the usual naval style; signal flags, ship's wheels, and paintings of battles adorning the walls. Down one entire side of the room, tables upon which trays of exotic food were perched caught his attention, and the ceiling was covered in layers of swirling gold leaf. Ahead of him in the room, there were roughly thirty people, obviously naval officers and their wives, milling idly about and sipping chilled wine. For a long moment, he was ignored entirely, and then an old man in an admiral's uniform caught sight of him. He was decked out extravagantly in all of his best clothes, the Star of the Order of Bath shining triumphantly from his breast alongside other medals of distinction. He broke off his conversation with a charming young woman in a yellow dress and moved to greet him.

"Ah, Captain West, I presume?" he asked delicately. West bowed.

"It is an honor, sir," he replied. The admiral bowed in turn.

"The honor, sir, is ours," he turned to the other assembled guests. "Ladies and gentlemen, it is my honor and pleasure to introduce to you the illustrious Captain West of the American Navy, our colleague recently arrived here aboard the sloop *Perseverance.*" There was a polite spattering of applause, as custom dictated, and West was greeted with eyes full of interest.

"I am First Lord of the Admiralty The Earl of St. Vincent, sir," the old man announced, turning back to West. "Please allow me to welcome you here to our dinner, and introduce the other guests."

Slowly but surely, the First Lord led West through the crowd, pointing out faces and prompting handshakes with all the assembled dignitaries. The Duke and Duchess of Kensington were in attendance, as were the Earls of Liverpool and Smallbridge. Admirals Hood, Cornwallis, and Southey were all "pleased to make West's acquaintance," and several of the more successful captains and commodores as well. Ambassador Edward was there, jovial as usual, and—

"There was one fellow particularly interested in you," said St. Vincent, with a wry smile, "But I'm not rightly certain where he is." West was not thrilled to meet another uniformed hero, dazed as he was by the jumble of new names and faces. He almost cried out in alarm when the First Lord finally spotted his quarry. "Ah! Bless my soul, he was here all along. Horatio!"

At that name, West's ears perked up, and his dulled senses sharpened rapidly, coming into focus as he was dragged towards the champagne table with an unmistakable urgency. His attitude was utterly changed. Could it be-?

The man to whom St. Vincent spoke was short; not overwhelmingly so, but short nonetheless. He wore a grey powdered wig, making his age hard to guess, but West put him somewhere in his fifties. There was a childish gleam in the eyes that stared out of the pleasant, interested face at West, and he inhaled sharply when the man made eye contact. The most striking thing about this man was the fact that his right sleeve was pinned, empty, to his uniform jacket.

"Captain West," said the First Lord. "Allow me to introduce Rear Admiral of the Blue Lord Sir Horatio Nelson. Horatio, this is American Captain Lowell West, the officer we've all heard so much about."

Nelson extended his left arm, and West took his hand. The grip was firm, but not hard. A thrill of excitement raced down West's spine as he shook the man's hand; this was Lord Nelson! The greatest naval genius of the age, and he was here, in this very room! As they unclasped, the little man spoke.

"Captain West! What a pleasure it is to meet you. Shall we talk about strategy, or will you be bored to tears? I dare say you've said quite enough on the subject already."

Nelson led West off into the crowd, rambling on about strategy and naval tactics and French food. They spoke for nearly half an hour, until finally the gathering was over, and the guests began to disperse.

"I had better not hold you prisoner much longer, Captain," said Nelson with a smile.

"It was a great pleasure speaking with you, milord," responded West, shaking his hand again in parting.

"I wish you the greatest success in the remainder of your career," Lord Nelson continued. "But for now, have a speedy journey home. Fair winds and following seas, Captain West."

"Thank you, Lord Nelson."

In the chaise on the return trip to the embassy, West could not help but smile the entire way.

But then it was down to business. He packed his things rapidly in his sea chest, sending it down to the dockyards at Plymouth to be loaded aboard the ship. He felt the same tense anticipation he'd had the first time he went aboard the old *Perseverance*. Bidding Ambassador Jay a final thanks for his hospitality and sending Tallis, who was to command *Perseverance*, a letter of farewell, he hailed another chaise at the corner and was off to the harbor.

Peering down through the forest of masts that towered from the water, past the ships of the line and vessels of war, he spotted her; the *United States*, flying the stars and stripes proudly amidst the sea of British ensigns. She was magnificent, the envy of every American captain and commodore, and, indeed, of many a King's officer as well. Her beautiful, sleek lines, adorned beakhead, and jet black hull betrayed her enormous speed and agility, while the painted white line running the length of her hull broken by forty-four gunports revealed her as a force to be reckoned with. She was certainly no sloop; with armament like that, she could engage nearly any other vessel that sailed the seas and find herself at no great disadvantage.

He disembarked from the carriage and summoned a shore boat to get out to her. Captains of smaller vessels nearby groaned with envy as he spoke her name to the boat's crew. He pulled out to her, coming up against her towering side rapidly and hauling himself up into the boarding rigging. The sideboys trilled their boatswain's pipes as he stepped aboard and saluted the first lieutenant, surveying the sprawling deck as he had only once before, at his meeting with Commodore Estleman in the Bay of Biscay. He read himself to the crew rapidly, as was formally required, and then set immediately about completing her stores and readying for sea. She was further along then his previous command had been; less remained to be taken aboard before departure.

Below, he discovered that the aft cabin was nearly twice as large as that of the *Perseverance* now that Estleman's possessions were gone. He arranged himself there, and then went up on deck again.

It seemed that the first lieutenant, a man called Peter Livingston, had everything well in hand. He was a seaman by every definition of the word, competent as far as his captain could see in most facets of sailing, an assumption backed up by the shipshape condition of the decks. It was a good thing, too, for a heavy frigate of this size and firepower would be a witch to handle in hurricane weather. The more junior lieutenants, Harries, second; Kettlewell, third; and Payson, fourth; seemed to have their strengths as well. It was a comfort to West, who was accustomed to having everything at sixes and sevens in the normal routine of a ship.

They worked late into the night completing stores, and then West retired a little past one o'clock.

He was nearly asleep before he remembered the mail. Livingston had mentioned a large envelope that had come for him earlier in the day. West lit his little candle and went to his desk to investigate.

There it was, bearing a royal seal and commission. Curious, he opened it.

Clerks Royal of the King
Palace of His Most Britannic Majesty

Captain Lowell West,

Under Express direction of the King himself, a Most Deserved Congratulations is to be offered to you upon the safe and speedy Execution of your Orders against Spain. You are Royally Commended for doing unto this nation a great Service in Conducting Safely the wife and daughter of the British Ambassador to Friendly Shores, and in Destroying the North Atlantic Fleet of our Enemy, freeing commerce between the United States and Great Britain.

Many years ago, for a similar naval Service, your forefather Robert West, was Knighted unto the Order of Bath. This title was revoked when your Father committed an Act of Treason in defending the United States during the Revolution. Because of your great Service to the King, I am instructed by His Majesty to restore unto you your Forefather's Title, Knight Commander of Bath.

God Save the King,
Sir Gideon Caldwell, Clerk

West set aside the letter and reached into the envelope again. Inside was a flat metallic object; upon inspection, it proved to be the distinctive medal of the Order of Bath, of the same type that the First Lord, and indeed, all of the naval officers at the recent luncheon wore. He was amazed to learn this of his grandfather, but not surprised. He proudly affixed the Star of Bath to the breast of his uniform, content finally that he could maintain a connection with Britain while continuing to serve his rightful homeland. He would not use the title "Sir Lowell West, K.C.B.," in his everyday life, though it would always be his option to do so; there was an incredible distaste for all titles of nobility in the United States as it was.

Feeling gratified and contented, West slipped pleasantly off to sleep.

He was awoken by a midshipman at five in the morning, and he knew, instantly, that this was it.

He went up on deck. The wind had borne round two points and increased by several knots, which was the reason he had been sent for. The salt breeze was blowing for the new world, and now was the time to catch it.

He looked back at the shore in the half darkness, seeing the silhouette of the many houses and government buildings that lined the dockyards, his eyes resting momentarily on Whitehall Steps at Admiralty. It had been refreshing to return to London again, but now it was time to go home.

The fresh breeze increased once more. West felt it swirl around him, beckoning him to his home shores once again after so long. It was time.

"Mr. Livingston," he called from his place on the quarterdeck.

"Sir?" replied the first lieutenant.

"Lay in a course to weather the island of Cuba," he ordered. They would sail directly out into the Atlantic at first, and then reach for those latitudes where the trade winds blew strong and steady, running straight to their destination from mid-ocean. Once resupplied, he would definitely be given a few weeks shore leave in Boston—to see his mother, to visit old Wilson—and then sent back down to the squadron or to Tripoli, to join the blockade. He did not care where he went, as long as he had a ship to captain and a wind behind him.

"Aye aye, sir," Livingston responded, nodding to the quartermaster at the con. A moment's pause.

"Set full sail, Mr. Livingston, and prepare to bring us out."

"Aye aye, sir."

That was that. Only a few moments later, the *United States* lurched joyfully to life under him, responding wonderfully to even the slightest press of canvas. She sailed past the towering H.M.S. *Victory* on her starboard side, rendering passing honors as they parted, and then there was the open ocean before them.

With the sun on his back, the breeze in his sails, and a fair wind and following sea to carry him to his destination, West stood confidently on his quarterdeck, certain that the ship under his feet would bear him wherever he had to go.

＊   ＊   ＊

There was a pause as the old man finished his story, looking out to sea once more. His pipe had gone out again, so he refilled it in the intervening silence, averting his eyes from mine as he remembered that command so many years ago.

"That's all there is to tell," he said, after a little while. "My career was solid, my reputation established. That's not to say it was easy from there, no!" he frowned slightly, then perked up again. "But that was my first success and possibly my greatest, the one that put me where I am today."

The mist had lifted from the Boston dockyards, and the sun was just beginning to pull itself above the horizon as Admiral Sir Lowell West and I finished our interview. I concluded the scribbling of notes in my little pad, closed it, and smiled up at him.

"Thank you for your time," I said, extending a hand. He took it, and I suddenly felt as he did at his meeting with Lord Nelson so many years ago. We shook hands heartily.

"It was my pleasure, Mr. Roberts," said he, rising with a groan. "Perhaps we shall meet again?"

"I hope so," I replied. "But for now, I have a lot of writing to do." He chuckled.

"Good luck with your book. I shall certainly read it the moment it is published."

"Thank you, sir."

"But for now, goodbye. I must be getting off to my home; my wife and son expected me half an hour ago." With that, he turned and strode purposefully off in the direction of the city lights, where smoke was beginning to rise from chimneys as people started their day.

I stood to watch him go, the sound of the ocean near at hand and the salty spray transporting me back to the days of Nelson's navy, back into that old man's memory.

I turned away from the harbor, pocketing my pen and paper and beginning the long walk home, reflecting on all that I had just heard. It would be quite a task to get it all down on paper. Somewhere behind me, a ship's bell clanged.

At that sound, I knew exactly what to write.

0-595-24783-0